POOR LITTLE RICH BOY

BY KATE SHERWOOD

This is a work of fiction. Names, characters, places, and events are either the product of the author's imagination or are used fictitiously, and any resemblance to actual persons, businesses, events, or locales is entirely coincidental.

Poor Little Rich Boy

Copyright © 2012 by Kate Sherwood

Cover Art by April Martinez

Copy Editing by Alicia Ramos

Print ISBN: 978-0-9881530-0-4

eBook ISBN: 978-0-9881530-1-1

http://www.katesherwoodbooks.com

PROLOGUE

"Is Alex already gone?" Nick Colton was too hung over to care about much, but his best friend's well-being was important enough to penetrate his misery.

Blake didn't respond. He yanked his keys out of his jacket pocket as he strode across the parking lot of the campus police station without acknowledging his son at all.

Nick stopped walking. "Alex," he said, as firmly as he could manage. "Is he already at home?"

Blake reached the silver Mercedes and dropped his clenched fist down onto the roof, knuckles showing white for several moments before his fingers relaxed. "Yes," he finally said.

"How come he got out so fast?" Nick started moving again, trying to ignore his roiling stomach as he headed for the passenger side of the car. "Or why did it take so long for me, I guess."

Blake pulled his door open and sank into the leather seat without answering. The silent treatment was getting old—though, given the state of Nick's head, it was nice that Blake wasn't yelling. Nick eased into his own seat, swallowing deeply to help settle his stomach after the slight descent and tried to think of something that would take his mind off his pain. He'd once counted his way through a hangover, reaching eighteen thousand, seven hundred and fifty before he'd given up and gotten on with his day. He didn't really want to do that again. Easier to think about Alex. It was always easy to think about Alex.

The car pulled out of the parking space and headed toward the street. "His parents came and got him?" Nick asked.

"I don't want to have this conversation right now." Blake's anger seemed to have faded into resignation.

"I don't need a conversation. I just want to be sure Alex is okay."

"You're so worried about him *now*," Blake said, amazement warring with bitterness in his tone. "But you didn't give him a second thought last night, did you?"

"What are you talking about?" Nick's confusion was genuine. "He's fine, isn't he?"

"Do you want to know why I took so long picking you up?" Blake pulled over and turned to look at his son.

"I *asked* you. So, yeah, I guess that means I'd like to know."

Blake looked annoyed at Nick's tone of voice, but stuck with his main topic. "I was in the Dean's office. I was trying to convince him not to expel my son, and not to revoke the scholarship of one of the most promising young men I've ever known."

"Revoke… they can't do that! Alex's grades are still really good! He works hard! Everybody blows off a little steam now and then; it's not a big deal. The Dean wasn't really going to revoke his scholarship, was he?" Nick didn't think the nausea he was feeling was completely hangover-related.

"'Blowing off steam'?" It sounded like Blake was developing some steam of his own. "That's what you call public drunkenness, vandalism, theft, and possession of a controlled substance? You call that 'blowing off steam'?"

"I call that a hell of a night," Nick said with a smirk. He knew the bravado wouldn't be appreciated, but that was half the fun. "You took care of it, right? You know Alex won't take money from us; if he loses that scholarship, he's screwed."

"I know that. You know that. We all know that. So why the *fuck* did you drag him along with you last night?" Blake rarely swore, which made this occasion that much more impressive.

Still, Nick refused to be intimidated. "I didn't drag him anywhere. He came because he wanted to."

"For a couple beers, maybe. Under-age drinking—that's not a big deal. But the rest of it? He *wanted* to get so drunk he could barely stand up, he *wanted* to rip all the reserved parking signs off and rearrange them, he *wanted* to steal two bicycles and ride them to the far side of campus, and he *wanted* to be caught with someone carrying a baggie of pot?"

"Well, he didn't want to get *caught*." Alex never wanted to get caught. But it didn't stop him from doing stuff. He was just more careful than Nick, usually.

"Alex doesn't smoke." It was a simple statement, with no room for doubt.

"He's tried it," Nick replied. "But, no, he doesn't like it much. The pot was mine, no question."

"No, there was no question." Blake stared through the windshield at the leafy campus and didn't say anything for quite a while. Finally, he turned back to look at Nick. "You didn't hear the part about you getting expelled? You have more history of trouble than Alex, and apparently you're on the verge of failing everything anyhow. The Dean said he appreciated my generous donations to the campus, but he couldn't let that appreciation get in the way of maintaining *some* sense of order."

"So… you made a bigger donation, right?" Nick wasn't going to play innocent; he knew what had happened. He'd done something stupid, and his father had bought his way out of it. That was the pattern they'd established over the years, and it seemed to work pretty well for everyone.

But this time, his father shook his head. "No," he said quietly.

Nick stared at him. "What? What do you mean? Come on, I'm not *expelled*. They wouldn't do that."

"Not quite yet." Blake was watching Nick with unusual intensity. "But they want *someone* to be punished. They can't just let this go, not after all the other crap you've pulled."

Nick was obviously expected to say something now, but he had no idea what. God, he wished he wasn't so hung over. "Is this— have you already sorted something out? Are you actually asking me something, or just trying to build up the drama before you tell me the deal you made?"

"You're nineteen. I can't legally make decisions for you. But, yes, I made a tentative deal with the Dean. He'll want you to sign something to show that you agree."

"Okay." This was sounding more familiar. Some sort of probation, maybe even community service. Nick had done community service before—it had been fun, actually, working at a day camp. He'd ended up going back for the rest of the summer, even after his hours were worked off; the kids had been excellent. Maybe he could go back there again. "So, what's the deal?"

"It's a package deal," Blake said quietly. "Alex gets to keep his scholarship. But you're out." It took the words a moment to register. "You can withdraw, rather than be expelled, if you want. They'll still be keeping a close eye on Alex, but I convinced them that without you around he'll be a model student."

"You... you sold me out? For the housekeeper's son?" Nick stopped as soon as the words were out of his mouth. He wouldn't apologize, but he hadn't meant that. He didn't give a good goddamn what Alex's mother did for a living. That wasn't the hurtful part of this. " *I'm* your—"He cut himself off again, swallowing hard as he realized that the moisture in his eyes wasn't just a blissful respite from the scratchiness of dehydration. But he wasn't going to cry about this. He hadn't cried for years, not since his mother. He sure as hell wasn't going to break that streak over this. The betrayal had just caught him by surprise.

Blake was back to looking out the windshield. Apparently he couldn't look his screw-up son in the eyes. "It's up to you. As I said, you'll have to sign a statement saying that this was your idea, agreeing that you have excessive influence over Alex, and taking full responsibility for the pot."

"And if I don't?" Nick had his rebellious body back under control and kept his voice light and insolent. He wasn't going to care about this. He wasn't going to let himself care about anything, not if he could help it.

"Then you'd stay in, do some community service, and Alex

would lose his scholarship."

"Can they do that? The scholarship was supposed to be based on grades, not behavior!"

"There are terms in the scholarship contract. A sort of morality clause. It's standard."

"So get the lawyers on it. This was the campus cops, Dad; I'm sure they screwed something up. They read us our rights, I think, but maybe we could make an argument that we were too drunk to understand. Something like that."

"It's not criminal charges, Nick. Not this time. It's not about whether they read you your rights." Blake sounded uncharacteristically tired. Nick couldn't figure out whether that meant he was winning or losing.

He pressed on. "So maybe that's what we argue. They're making decisions that are just as serious as criminal charges would be, and they're doing it without due process. I don't know. The lawyers will figure something—"

"No." Blake's hands were gripping the steering wheel as if it were able to control the direction of the conversation. "I'm not hiring lawyers. I'm not letting you squirm out of this. I've done that too often." He turned toward Nick, and he looked exhausted. Worn out and old, not the powerhouse Nick was used to. "I've made a lot of mistakes, Nick. I know that. After your mother died, I was so…" He frowned as if remembering the pain and confusion, then shook his head. "I didn't help you as much as I should have. And I've let you run too wild since then, let you get away with too much. But that has to stop. It stops now."

Blake shouldn't have mentioned Nick's mother. They *never* talked about her, and Nick wasn't sure he could forgive the violation. "What if I don't go along with it?" He leaned back against his door and raised his eyebrows insolently. "What if I say it was all Alex's idea? You'd hang *me* out to dry; I guess that shouldn't surprise me. But you wouldn't do that to Alex. If he was going to lose his scholarship, you'd fight for him, even if it meant hauling me up along with him."

Blake didn't answer right away, and when he did, it felt like he was speaking from somewhere far away. "You know what I tell people about you? When they say negative things, or think I should be stricter with you? I tell them that you're a bit wild, and you can be a bit of an ass, sometimes. But I tell them you've got a big heart, underneath it all. A *good* heart." He frowned. "I need that to be true. If that's not true, if you're not a loving human being, deep down, then what the hell have I done? What have I raised?"

"You take credit for raising Alex, don't you? I don't know how his *real* father feels about that, but we both know you've always thought of Alex as a son. The son you could actually be proud of." Nick felt his lip curl into a snarl. "So even if I'm some sort of monster, you'll still have Alex."

"I don't think you're a monster, Nick. But I think it's time for you to start proving it."

"By taking the fall for this. By rolling over and taking some bullshit punishment for a little stupid fun. Is this a test? Or just a joke? Is there a hidden camera in the back seat?"

"It's no joke. You have a choice to make; you'd better think about what you want to do. The Dean wants to see you first thing tomorrow, though, so you don't have all that much time."

"The Dean can kiss my ass. I'll see him when I'm ready." The bravado was childish, but satisfying. "Now, can you drive, please? I want to talk to Alex."

Blake looked like he had something more to say, but after a moment he put the car into gear and pulled away from the curb. They drove the rest of the way home in silence.

"It's for the best, Alejandro." Rosa Díaz was a proud woman, but she sounded like she was pleading. Right there in her own kitchen, the place she normally ruled with an iron fist. Alex didn't know if he could stand it. "It's best for both of you. You'll be able to concentrate on your studies. And Nicky can…" She reached over and gripped Alex's hand. "He can figure out what he wants to do. He needs some time to grow up a little, I think."

"I can't do it." Alex pulled his hand away from his mother's. "He's my best friend. He's…" They'd had the conversation almost a year ago, Alex confessing to his mother before working up to telling the whole family. But it was still hard to put it into words. "He's more than that. I love him."

"Are you proud of him? Do you respect him?" Rosa sighed and leaned back a little. "I love him, too, you know. Ever since you two were little boys, both so sweet and good. I love him almost as much as my own babies. But he's *al garete*, Alejandro. Adrift. He's been that way for years, but he used to let you tow him in the right direction. But lately, he's been towing you. He's been dragging you off course."

Alex didn't know how to respond. He knew his mother was right in all the details, but he couldn't accept her conclusion. He *needed* Nick. Not just his body, though that had certainly become an important part of their relationship over the last few years. No, it was all of him: his quick mind, his laughing eyes, the sweet smile that was just for Alex; the years they'd shared, the trust they'd built. Nick was a part of Alex, just as Alex was a part of Nick. It was impossible to think of losing that.

"Mr. Colton agrees," Rosa said quietly. "Not for you, but for Nick. He's worried that the boy will never grow up, never figure out what he wants to be. You've seen men like that, Alejandro. So much money, and so little sense. Their lives are empty, and they try to fill the space with their alcohol and drugs and stupid toys. They don't value anything because they haven't ever had to earn anything. And that's what Mr. Colton thinks Nick could turn into, if we don't do something." She reached for Alex's hand again, and this time he let her hold on. "It's what *I* think he could turn into. If things go on as they have been."

"He's a good person." It sounded insufficient, even to Alex's ears.

"He's a little boy. And he's showing no interest in turning into a man." Rosa stood up. "We've tried everything, Alex. Nothing matters to him."

"*I* matter to him. And so do you. So does his father. I know they fight, but Nick cares about him."

"Not enough, apparently." Rosa had started pacing, measuring the confines of the small kitchen. "He doesn't listen to anyone! He does whatever he wants, even when he knows it's stupid. Maybe he likes it even better then. He's looking for…" She paused, then threw her hands up in disgust. "I don't know what he's looking for, but he hasn't found it anywhere around here." She turned and looked at Alex with an expression full of love and sympathy. "I'm sorry, *mi tesoro*, but he hasn't found it with you."

Alex stood so quickly he almost knocked her over. Once upright, he wasn't sure what he wanted to do. He just couldn't be there anymore, couldn't listen to any more of his mother's cruel words wrapped in loving tones. "I'm going out," he managed to say, and headed for the door. The first breath of cool outdoor air let him clear his head enough to figure out where he wanted to be.

At the first sight of his bike in the garage, Alex wanted to kick it, destroy it, curse it for not being available when it had been needed. His environmentalism combined with his limited budget to keep him from owning a car, and the loss of a high school classmate had made Nick careful about not driving after drinking. The bike should have been Alex's transportation of choice. If he had ridden it to school instead of taking the bus, they wouldn't have needed to take the bikes the night before, and all this could have been avoided. He stopped himself. *Needed* to take the bikes? He and Nick had *needed* to steal someone else's property, because they'd *needed* to get across campus faster because… because nothing. Because Nick had thought it would be funny, and Alex had gone along with Nick, just like he always did.

"Maybe it's not him." Janissa's voice was quiet, but Alex still jumped. His sister was like that, gliding around silently and then saying things that were far too close to his own thoughts.

"Go away, Jani." Alex pulled the bike away from the wall, but there was something tangled in its spokes and he had to bend over to figure it out.

"Not you, either. Maybe it's the two of you together. Maybe it just doesn't work, at least right now."

"Jani, seriously, fuck off. I'm not in the mood for your psychic bullshit."

"I was sitting on the stairs, asshole; I heard the whole conversation. And I heard Mami and Papi last night. They were both crying, Alex."

Alex yanked the bike free from the tines of the rake that had been restraining it. But Jani had used the time to slide around so she stood between him and the door. She was two years younger than he, and slightly built. He could easily have pushed her aside, but he hadn't touched his sister in anger since he'd made her cry at her seventh birthday party. Besides, she was his biggest ally in the family, and she loved Nick almost as much as Alex did. She'd understand how impossible it was to even think of giving him up. Or she *should* understand. "What are you saying? What do you think I should do?"

"I have no idea. But you should remember how much they've sacrificed so you could have this chance. They both work so hard, and you know Papi could use your help with the business, but he hardly ever asks. They both tiptoe around when you're studying, and yell at us not to bother you. It's not just *your* scholarship, you know?"

"I don't care about that. I care about *Nick*."

"And does that seem right to you? That you're ignoring your whole future for some guy? Your whole family? I get it, Alex... it's *Nick*. But where is this going? He's got money. If he flunks out of school, he'll just sit around and laugh about it. But this is your big chance. This matters to you—and that means it should matter to him. If it doesn't..." She paused, then stepped aside so he could pass by. "I don't know. If it doesn't matter to him, I just don't know."

Alex didn't know either. He didn't have any idea what the hell he was supposed to do with any of this. He needed to get out of there. He pushed the bike out of the garage and pedaled off down the alley.

It was early afternoon by the time Nick made it to the beach. After they got home there'd been a bit more fighting, and then he'd needed to talk his dad into loaning him a car since his own was still parked outside the frat house on campus. "You know where I'm going, Dad. You know I need to talk to him. Why are you being so pissy about this?"

His father had eventually given in, and Nick had driven the SUV to the Díaz home. The welcome he received was much cooler than he had come to expect, and he wasn't sorry to hear that Alex wasn't there. The Díazes hadn't known where Alex had gone, but Nick had a pretty good idea.

So he'd headed for their spot at the beach, a rocky point where the land met the water. Nick jogged down the familiar path through the park and broke off into the forest where they always did. It wasn't far from there. The huge old tree, the flat rock at its base, looking out over the water. And Alex, leaning against the trunk, staring at Puget Sound as if it were about to disclose the mysteries of the universe. Nick's shoulders relaxed as soon as he saw Alex. Everything would be fine, now.

"Hey, man," he said softly, and Alex jerked his head around. He looked almost guilty. There was no reason for that, though, and Nick smiled as he moved forward. "Last night kind of got out of hand, huh? But it'll be okay. My dad's got it fixed up. Your scholarship is still fine." Nick hadn't realized he'd made his decision until he saw Alex in person. Of course he'd take the blame. It was mostly his fault, after all. He hadn't forced Alex into anything, but Alex would have been at home studying if Nick hadn't invited him out. And Alex cared about school a hell of a lot more than Nick did.

"It's no big deal," Nick continued when he saw that the strange expression hadn't faded from Alex's face. "Everything's good." He flopped down on the ground next to Alex and leaned in for the kiss that had become their standard greeting. But Alex leaned away.

"Are you mad?" Nick cast his mind over the night before. There were some fuzzy details toward the end, but Alex had seemed friendly enough in the police car. Scared, and frustrated at being too drunk to deal with the situation, but not angry. "Did something happen?"

"Did something happen?" Alex repeated in amazement. "We got arrested. We almost got kicked out of school. My parents had to come pick me up from the police station after I spent the night in a cell. Yeah, Nick, *something happened*."

Alex could be wound pretty tight, sometimes. Nick thought about reaching out and trying to massage some of the tension out of Alex's shoulders, but it didn't seem like that would go over very well. "Okay, that wasn't so good. But it's over now, right? It's all taken care of. You're fine. Right?"

"So everything just goes back to normal? We just forget about it, do the same thing again, and see if we get away with it again?"

"We didn't really get away with it *this* time. *You* did, I guess, but—"

"I got away with it? Jesus, did you hear what I just said? My parents were crying last night, Nick. Because of me. Us. Because we did something really stupid." He jerked to his feet, his lean body tense and angry. He whirled around to stare at Nick, and for a moment it felt like Alex was maybe going to start swinging. Nick decided he'd take one hit, then cover up and hope Alex stopped. There was no way he could fight back. He'd never do anything to hurt Alex.

But Alex's face softened as he stared, shifting from anger to heartbreaking sadness. "This isn't good, Nick. You and me. It's not good."

Nick felt the breath rush out of him and wished it had just been a punch. "What do you mean?" he managed to ask. "You and me? We're great. We're the only thing that *is* good."

"That's how it feels when we're together," Alex admitted. "But sooner or later we have to deal with the rest of the world, and that's when it all falls apart."

"You're overreacting." He had to be. Nick wouldn't accept anything else. "It was a bad night. You're still hung over, right? Everything seems worse when you're hung over. Come on—I'll drive you home, you can have a nap, and everything will be good when you wake up."

But Alex didn't move. "It's like a drug. *You're* like a drug. And I'm addicted. It's great while I'm high, but it's not real. It's not healthy."

The panic was rising from Nick's gut and pressing against his ribs, his throat. His heart. But he fought it down and smiled. "You've been listening to too much '80s pop. Nobody's addicted to love, love isn't a drug, and it doesn't have a bad name. Settle down, Alex."

"I can't see you anymore."

No. Nick refused to hear the words. "You're freaking me out, here. Come on back to the car. Maybe not straight home—you want to get something to eat, first? Salty fat, that's what's good for a hangover. Or carbs. Maybe salty, fatty carbs. French fries. We should go get some fries, okay? And a smoothie. With bananas. Potassium. We'll get you rehydrated and set back up, and this will all go away. And I'll be more careful about stuff. I'll make sure you have more time to study, and—"

"I can't do it. Nick, I can't. It's not…" Alex took a deep, shaky breath and stared at Nick as if trying to send him a telepathic message. "It's not good for me. I love you, but *you're* not good for me."

If Alex had been looking for magic words, he'd found them. Nick wasn't good for Alex. Being around Nick *hurt* Alex. "I don't…" *I don't want to hurt you. Not ever.* "I don't understand. Is this…" He wasn't sure he could say the words, but he forced them through jaws that were trying not to scream. "Is this forever?"

Alex's eyes were wide. He looked just as terrified as Nick felt. "I don't know. I think so," he whispered. "I mean… I think we have to think of it that way."

Maybe Alex had more to say, but Nick wasn't there to hear it. He was crashing through the undergrowth, fighting his way to the path with vision blurred by something he refused to call tears. He didn't need Alex. He didn't need anyone. He made it to the SUV and pulled himself inside. He probably wasn't in any shape to drive, but he couldn't stand the idea of Alex coming after him and seeing him this way.

He slammed the vehicle into gear and pulled out of the parking lot with a spray of gravel. It felt good to be driving. He was in control of the vehicle, in control of his life. Instead of taking the turn toward home, he kept driving and got on I-5, heading south. He had no idea where he was going; he was just getting away. Away from Alex, away from his father, away from Seattle.

It would be more than a decade before he returned.

CHAPTER ONE

Even after so long away, even with the exhaust fumes and the food court and all the other intrusions of the airport, Seattle still smelled like home. Nick clamped down tightly on that idea and pushed it into the corner of his mind where he stored unwelcome sentimentality. New York was home. Or Los Angeles. London, Paris, Tokyo, Mumbai. He didn't have a home, really. And that was fine. He didn't need one.

He found the waiting car and sank into the soft leather upholstery as the driver supervised the transfer of his bags to the trunk. The tinted windows helped a little, shutting out the invasive gazes of bystanders and giving Nick a little privacy, but it wasn't enough. He was still tense, more than he could remember being in a long time. Probably since he left Seattle to begin with. Maybe *that* was the familiar Seattle smell, some sort of stress-produced hormone oozing out of Nick's own skin.

Not that there hadn't been good times. But he pushed those memories away with practiced efficiency. The past was the past, for good or bad, and he needed to focus on the present. This trip was important, the culmination of years of work, and he couldn't allow any distractions.

He rolled his shoulders, took a deep breath and released it, purposely tensed his muscles and then concentrated on letting them relax. But the tricks Liam had taught him didn't work. Damn, maybe he should have let Liam come along after all. It could have added another layer of surreality to what was already destined to be an awkward situation. He quickly keyed his phone, and when Liam picked up Nick said, "Can you set up a massage for me at the Four Seasons? Do you know somebody out here?"

"Nobody as good as me, babe. You need to be in New York for true quality. And no happy endings! That is *not* a standard service for professional massage therapists."

"Oh. Well, never mind then. That's really all I was looking for." Nick kept his voice serious, and waited for Liam's outraged response.

Instead, Liam's smile was audible as he said, "You're pretty tense, huh? You sure you don't want me to come out? I could shuffle my appointments and be on the next flight."

Of course he could. Liam was always more than ready to accommodate Nick's needs. It wasn't out of love, of course. There was affection, maybe, but really they shared a mutual understanding: Nick had money, and Liam appreciated that. Liam was good-looking, socially acceptable, and sexually adventurous, and Nick appreciated all these qualities. Though they'd never discussed it, they were both aware that Liam had his eyes on something less temporary and more lucrative than their current relationship. Nick was far too young to be somebody's sugar daddy, but he made sure Liam enjoyed enough fringe benefits to keep him compliant. A few tropical vacations a year and the occasional shopping spree were sufficient, for now. For the future, well… Nick planned ahead in his business life, but he preferred to maintain flexibility in the personal sphere.

"You'd be too much of a distraction," he said into the phone. The car was moving now, and he tried to focus on the conversation as a way to avoid looking for familiar landmarks. "You know how hard it is for me to ignore you. But it'd be nice to get some kinks worked out. You can find a masseuse, if it makes you feel better. Just make sure she has strong hands."

"A licensed massage therapist, you mean."

"Yeah, I'm definitely going to check for a license. This body is a finely tuned precision machine. I can't let just anyone adjust my chassis."

"Do you even know what a chassis is?"

"I know more than you do, I'll bet." Nick glanced outside, then caught himself and returned his gaze to the rich interior of the vehicle. There was a television embedded in one wall and he hit buttons until a movie popped up. He had no idea what it was, and didn't really care. Beautiful people running around in fancy dresses.

Fine. Something for him to look at. "If you're not up to the challenge, I can talk to the concierge. Hell, the front-desk clerk can probably hook me up. I just thought you might like to consult."

"I'm on the website now," Liam replied. "You want in-room, I suppose? Lord knows you couldn't be expected to relax in a semi-public environment." A few clicks, and then, "Oooh, this sounds interesting... avocado, lime blossom, and ginger! For your scalp! I think you'll like that."

"You think I'll like having food in my hair?"

"Yes. Yes, I do." Liam was clearly distracted by the online shopping opportunities. "Now, do you feel more like Alpine, Swedish, or Aromatherapy, for the massage portion?"

"The whole point of calling you was so I wouldn't have to make these decisions."

"And to hear my melodious voice." Liam waited expectantly.

"Yeah, that too. But seriously, I don't care what kind of massage. Just something that will let me sleep tonight."

"I told you to take some of my pills with you. You'd like them, if you'd just give them a try! Sleep like a baby and wake up totally refreshed, not groggy at all."

"I don't need drugs to go to sleep. Pick a massage, will you?" The conversation was getting irritating.

"I'll call and speak to them. There are too many variables for me to make a firm choice yet."

"Set it up to be daily, okay? Say, ten o'clock every night? Not the avocado thing, just the massage."

"They're going to charge extra for late night." Liam's voice gentled. "You really think you're going to need that? You're *sure* you don't want me out there?"

Nick looked out the window and saw nothing but highway and trees. Generic scenery that he could have found practically anywhere on the continent. Nothing to worry about. "No, I'm fine. But if things go well, maybe we should go somewhere afterward. I'm already halfway to Hawaii—you could fly out and meet me and we could go the rest of the way together, maybe. Sound good?"

"You know how much I love Hawaii, babe." Liam sounded satisfied; his offers had earned him the reward he was seeking. "What's the timeline on that?"

"Hopefully less than a week here. And as long as you give me some time to work, we can be in Hawaii for a week or so after that."

"Sounds great. Should I book something?"

"No, not yet. The dates aren't firm." Maybe Nick shouldn't have mentioned it. But Liam wouldn't be too disappointed if it didn't work out; he was used to Nick's demanding schedule. And he'd been hinting that he needed a new watch. If Nick spent enough on that, the vacation wouldn't be missed at all. "Okay, so you'll set something up with the hotel? That's taken care of?"

"Absolutely. I'll get you the second-best massage you've ever had."

"Thanks. I'll talk to you later." Nick hung up, and immediately regretted it. He could have listened to Liam a little longer, could have hinted at a few more extravagant gifts. Jesus, he would have bought the bastard an East Side condo if it meant a way out of the next conversation.

But that was stupid. This conversation was the start of the payoff. It was the whole reason Nick was in Seattle, and he'd been looking forward to it for years. Why the hell was he being reluctant now?

He took a deep breath and punched the barely remembered number into his phone. A familiar voice answered, but not the one he'd been expecting. He was tempted to hang up, but stopped himself in time. He wasn't here to hide. He made his voice relax as he said, "Hi, Rosa. It's Nick. Is my father available?"

They'd all gathered in the sunroom, enjoying the rare spring sunshine without braving the cool winds, trying to pretend it was just another casual afternoon. The Díazes didn't usually socialize too much with the Coltons; they all got along, but it was awkward. Strange for Rosa to sit and eat the hors d'oeuvres she would normally have been in charge of preparing. But the families had been entwined for long enough that they'd gotten fairly good at pretending. The pretense was destroyed as soon as the phone rang and all eyes turned to the handset sitting between Blake and Rosa. She waited for him to pick it up, but he gestured nervously for her to do it.

"Hello, Colton residence," she said in her softly accented voice, and then waited while someone spoke on the other end. "It's good to hear your voice, Nick. Your father's right here." She extended the phone, and Blake took a deep breath before accepting it and lifting it to his head.

"Nick!" His voice was full of false cheer, nearly pathetic bonhomie, but Alex didn't think he'd have been able to do any better himself. "You're in town? Your flight was okay?" A short pause, and then, "And where are you now? We'd talked about dinner, but you weren't sure what time you'd be in. But you're early enough. You could come over here, or we could meet at a restaurant, if you'd rather." Another pause, and Alex didn't want to watch Blake's face as his brittle hopefulness faded into something much more quiet. "Of course. We understand. But we would really like to see you, son. It's a terrible situation that's brought you back, but that doesn't mean no good can come of it." He looked over at Adrianna Colton, curled up lethargically next to her mother, her blue hospital mask almost matching the color of her tired eyes. "A *lot* of good, we hope. For Anna, of course, but for all of us. For you and the whole family. That's what I'm hoping for." Another short pause. "Okay. We'll see you tomorrow, then, at the hospital. You have all the information? Everything you need? And you're fine tonight, there's nothing we can do?" He pinched the bridge of his nose, then said, "Okay. Sleep well, Nick. We'll see you tomorrow."

Blake held the phone in his hand for quite a while after the call ended. Then he looked up at the assembled group and forced another smile onto his face. "He can't make it for dinner. He says he has some business to take care of, and he's just flown in from Hamburg, so he's jet-lagged as well. But we'll see him at the doctor's tomorrow. Helena and I will. And we'll try to…" He broke off, then stood abruptly and strode out of the room. Helena, the stepmother Nick had never met, gently disengaged herself from Adrianna and followed him.

"*Hijo de la gran puta,*" Alex's father said softly. "Nick's going to make him crawl?"

Alex looked pointedly at Adrianna and her little brother Damon, who had eased into his mother's place and was trying to interest his sister in a toy car. "We don't know that," he said. "Maybe he really is tired. Maybe he's just feeling… shy? Tentative? It's been a long time for him, too, and there have been a lot of changes."

"Shy and tentative?" Alex's father snorted. "Are we talking about the same Nick Colton we all used to know?"

"Well, no, we probably aren't." Alex tried to sound reasonable, finding the same tone that worked so well for him in negotiations at work. "It's been more than ten years. He's obviously changed. If only by not once asking his father for money."

"He emptied his trust fund the day he turned twenty-one," Andrés countered. Alex's father had always liked Nick well enough, but had never loved him like the rest of the family did. And now he was in Puerto Rican patriarch mode, ready to defend his loved ones against an outside threat. Difficult for him, since his loved ones seemed intent on bringing the threat back into the fold at the earliest opportunity. Alex would have liked to sympathize, but he had seen the hope in his mother's eyes and would rather support that than help his father.

And Alex had good arguments to use. "It was only a couple hundred thousand. How long would the Nick you knew have lived on that much? And what was he doing for money *before* he turned twenty-one?"

"If he'd been using his credit cards, maybe we wouldn't all have thought he was dead in a ditch somewhere," Andrés growled. "I wouldn't put it past him to have done that deliberately, cackling away at the thought of all of us sick with worry."

Alex had never heard Nick cackle in his life, but didn't think that was a point worth addressing. "Or maybe he was trying to be independent and responsible. That's what you all wanted from him, right? So he did it, and all of a sudden that's wrong, too!"

"He sent the cards," Rosa said softly. The Christmas cards. The first one had been like a message from above, all of them gathering around to read it over and over again, searching for hints or subtext. The message had been cool and almost formal, a simple greeting and wishes for a happy new year, and the envelope had been addressed to "Blake Colton and the Díaz family," as if they were all equally important, or, more to the point, equally insignificant to Nick. So, yes, a bit of a message there, but the most important thing had been that Nick was okay. And every year after that, another card. Just enough to maintain a tiny thread of contact. And, while the cards hadn't had return addresses, the postmark on the most recent missive had been enough to help the private detectives track Nick down when it became clear that he might be Adrianna's last hope.

"He didn't have to come in person," Alex said. Everything else was a rehash of discussions the family'd had countless times before, but the visit was new. "He could have been tested in New York. Could have done the donation there, too, if it turns out that he's a match. The transplant isn't his reason for coming, it's just his excuse. He's here for something else—he has to be."

Marta's fingers were warm and strong as they slipped around his. She and Alex had been together for several years, and she was as comfortable in the Colton home as any of the Díaz family. "I know you want that to be true, sweetie. And I really hope it is. But don't get too excited, okay? Like you said, you don't really know him anymore. It's hard for you to be sure about his motivations for any of this. I just don't want to see you disappointed."

He smiled and squeezed her fingers. She was right, he supposed. But she didn't know Nick. And she didn't understand Nick and Alex. It was a good line, saying that they didn't know Nick anymore, but Alex didn't even believe it himself. He knew Nick. It felt like they'd been joined at a cellular level or something, a bond that couldn't ever fade. It could change. The way they expressed it, at least, had changed. He looked at Marta's blonde perfection and thought about Nick. He'd never really noticed how similar their coloring was. Everyone had seen the likeness between Adrianna and the baby pictures of Nick that still hung in the long upstairs hallway of the Colton residence. It had been one of the things that had given them hope about a possible genetic match. But no one had ever mentioned a similarity between Nick and *Marta*. Probably it was just in Alex's imagination.

Marta snuggled in closer to him, her body warm and comforting, and Alex put an arm around her. She had a way of holding their hands together so that her diamond engagement ring was always on the outside, always on display. As he looked at it now, Alex ignored the familiar stir of anxiety. He had a good career, and he'd helped get his younger siblings set up in life. He was engaged to a beautiful, kind, intelligent woman. His life was on track. He was doing everything he was supposed to do. But now, Nick Colton was back in town, and Alex had no idea what the hell was going to happen. It was frightening, but there was a tiny twist down in Alex's gut, in an area he generally tried to ignore; a twist that reminded him that Nick's return was exciting, as well.

CHAPTER TWO

Nick made sure he was a little late to the doctor's appointment. He didn't want to sit around in a waiting room making awkward small talk. But when he pushed the glass door open and saw his father's expression, he regretted his decision. It was clear in the older man's face: Blake had thought Nick wasn't going to show.

Nick's guilt turned to resentment almost immediately. Ten minutes late, and that was enough to blow any faith Blake had in his son's integrity. Good to know. He put on a breezy smile and extended his hand. "Sorry I'm late—traffic." Nick had seen photos of his father in business magazines and corporate newsletters, so there were no surprises in his appearance. And he'd seen the woman beside his father, too, always carefully posed as the perfect wife. "You must be Helena. It's nice to meet you. I'm sorry it's under such bad circumstances." He smiled, calm and in control, and turned to the nurse behind her half-wall and sliding glass. "I'm Nick Colton. I have an appointment."

She nodded efficiently and returned his smile. "I'll let the doctor know you're here."

"They're going to take blood." Blake sounded nervous but determined to give Nick what information he had. "Quite a bit of it. They need to do a lot of different tests. Adrianna—Anna—was home for a visit yesterday, but we had to bring her back last night. She's very sick. We don't have a lot of time, so they're going to be rushing you through the process as quickly as they can. Compressed timelines. You understand."

"That's fine. I appreciate efficiency." Nick tried another smile, and his father tentatively returned it.

His wife, though, didn't seem convinced. "Would you like to see her? She's just a couple floors down. I'm sure she'd like to meet her big brother."

That didn't sound like a good idea. "Maybe after we finish up here, if there's time. I have a lunch meeting scheduled, and then I'm booked all afternoon."

Blake looked curious. "What sort of business are you in? You're looking at doing work in Seattle?"

"Maybe. I do a lot of entrepreneurial stuff—venture capital, corporate restructurings. That sort of thing."

"That sounds interesting." Blake might have had more to say, but the nurse leaned over her desk and caught Nick's eye.

"The doctor's ready for you. You can come around the side over there." She gestured, and Nick moved.

But his father caught his arm, releasing his grip almost as quickly as he'd grabbed hold. "Do you want me to come with you?"

That was cute, like Nick was a little boy. But Blake hadn't been there when Nick was a child, and Nick certainly didn't need him now. "No, I'll be fine. You guys should go visit your daughter; I've got your cell number, if we need to get hold of you."

"After the doctor… well, after your lunch, and your meetings… we should get together. Just drinks, if you can't make dinner. We can get caught up."

Nick had thought he was going to enjoy this, but now that it was all happening he just wanted it to be over with. "Tonight's not good, actually. I'm right in the middle of something pretty big. And you must have a lot of family stuff to be dealing with. A sick daughter, and the other kid probably needs lots of attention too, right?"

"The other kid? Your brother?" Helena said acidly. "Damon? He's five, and he loves dinosaurs and soccer. In case you were wondering."

"I wasn't, really, but I'll keep that in mind." Nick gave her an artificially cautious look, as if suggesting that she was completely irrational. "Is there more important information you'd like to share, or is it okay with you if I go talk to a doctor about the possibility of a painful and invasive medical procedure that might help save your daughter's life?"

"Your *sister's* life." She jutted her jaw out stubbornly, dark hair and blue eyes and the same damn bone structure, the same skin tone... Nick wasn't going to think about that, wasn't going to let himself acknowledge how much she looked like his mother. "She's not just *our daughter*. She's your sister."

"So you keep saying," he agreed with a bland smile. "And I think I'm doing what you want in that regard—getting tested. So everyone's happy, right?" He nodded in dismissal and turned to follow the nurse down a long hallway to a small examination room. He was pretty sure his father and Helena stood and watched him go, but he wasn't even tempted to turn around and check.

The doctor was a middle-aged brown-skinned man, portly but not quite fat. He smiled happily at Nick and said, "Thank you for coming, Mr. Colton. I'm Doctor Chutani. We're going to take some blood today, and I'm going to ask you some basic questions. If we find that you're a good match, we'll perform further tests, including a full physical. We'll also ask you to watch a short film and read some information about what would be involved in becoming a bone-marrow donor. We'll be available to answer questions at any time." His eyes crinkled as if he'd told a joke and he said, "Do you have any questions so far?"

"No, not yet."

"Excellent." He picked up a clipboard from the nearby counter. "So… any existing medical conditions?" He ran through an almost dizzying list of possible illnesses, and Nick was happy to shake his head for each one. The list of countries visited was a bit more difficult, but the doctor seemed mostly concerned with actual residence time, not short visits, so Nick was fine. Then, out of the blue, "Have you had sex with another man since 1977?" the doctor asked, his voice as neutral as it had been for all the other questions, his eyes still locked on the clipboard as if it held the secrets to all of life's mysteries.

"What?" Nick was genuinely taken by surprise. "1977? I wasn't even alive in 1977."

"No. But the human immunodeficiency virus was."

"You don't take donations from anyone who's had sex with a man since *1977*? Because of HIV?"

"Not from any *man* who's had sex with a man, no. Some guidelines say that it's only any time in the last five years, but we're a bit more careful, here."

"Or a bit more discriminatory. Damn, I had no idea that was a criterion." He tried to think it through. "What's the risk? You guys test for HIV, don't you? You should be testing for all kinds of crap."

"We do. But the tests aren't 100% accurate, so we also screen our candidates very closely."

"Wow. But the kid's pretty desperate, isn't she? I mean, from what I'm hearing, it sounds like she's more or less done for without the transplant. You guys would honestly turn down a viable, HIV-negative donor just because he had sex with a man in 1978?"

"Those are the rules of the hospital, yes." Doctor Chutani's voice was still neutral, but he was looking at Nick now, his eyes intelligent but inscrutable. "I need an answer to the question. Have you had sex with another man since 1977?"

Nick had never hidden his sexual orientation. At first, his openness had been one more act of rebellion, another refusal to act the way he was expected to. But eventually it had become a point of pride. He had never hidden who he was, and if people didn't like it, that was their problem. Damn, this could be his way out of the whole thing. Tell the truth to the doctor and point it out to Blake and the self-righteous new wife, and then get back to the real reason he was in town, without all this distraction. That would be the easy option. But Nick felt his head shaking side to side even before the words came out of his mouth. "No. I haven't." Strange for a lie to feel so virtuous.

The doctor paused thoughtfully, then nodded and went on with his questions. A technician came in and took endless vials of blood, and that was all. The doctor asked Nick to check in with the nurse on the way out to make sure that the hospital still had his current contact information, and escorted Nick back to the hall. It seemed strange to have it all over with so quickly. A child's life was at stake—shouldn't there have been something more dramatic?

Nick made his way to the front of the hospital and was just about to raise his hand to hail a cab. Then he stopped. He turned back to the hospital and peered inside. There had to be one; there always was. He had no idea why, but he turned back and headed for the door. The gift shop was just inside the main lobby, a bright splash of color against the more sterile surroundings. Nick looked around the place and found himself completely bewildered. Luckily, he was good at delegating.

"Excuse me," he said to the teenage girl behind the counter. "I need something for a little girl. She's about seven? Maybe eight. And I think maybe she's got a suppressed immune system. Does that matter? Can she still have toys?"

"They're pretty good about sterilizing things, upstairs. And sometimes it's nice for kids to get presents they can't have yet for when they get out of the hospital. You know… one more thing for them to look forward to."

That was a bit more wisdom than he'd expected from this kid. "Okay, well… let 'er rip, then. Maybe an assortment, some she can have now, and some she can have when she gets out?"

The girl smiled and guided Nick toward a pink display shelf. This felt oddly risky, but surely it wouldn't hurt to make a friendly gesture. "And while we're at it," he added, "I don't suppose you have anything with soccer? Or dinosaurs? Dinosaurs *playing* soccer would be pretty much ideal, I guess. Anything like that?"

"Not quite," the girl said with a smile, "but I'm sure we can find something that will work."

"What the hell is Nick Colton up to?" George Tarkinson had never been a fan of small talk, and Alex was accustomed to scrambling to orient himself when they spoke. But this time Alex actually wondered whether his phone had somehow cut out the first part of the conversation, because George was making no sense at all.

He leaned back in his desk chair and stared at the speakerphone. "What do you mean? He's in town for some family stuff." Blake wanted his personal life kept separate from his business as much as possible, and Alex tried to respect that. But he seemed to be the go-to guy for shareholders seeking information about their CEO, so it wasn't always easy to be discreet. "I'm surprised you even know about his visit."

"Family stuff? Is that why he's invited me and a bunch of other board members to a dinner tonight? Three days before the AGM?"

Alex thought as quickly as he could, but wasn't fast enough. He had to say something... "I don't know about that, George. That's... you're right, that doesn't sound like something related to..." Related to the reason Nick had *said* he was in town. But as Alex himself had pointed out, there was really no need for Nick to have flown across the continent for a blood test. Alex had assumed the other reason was a desire to reconnect with his family, but maybe Alex had been naïve. "Did he not tell you anything else? He just called out of the blue and asked you to dinner?"

"Said he had a business proposition, but wouldn't go into details. He's shelling out for *Delilah's*, too, so I guess whatever he's got on his mind, he's taking it pretty seriously. Unless he's planning to stick us with the bill."

"And it's not just you? He called other board members as well?"

"I've talked to three others. There aren't that many of us with significant holdings, so if he's talked to me and three others, he's probably talked to us all. I thought you'd know what was going on. You two were always tight when you were kids."

SeaCo Toys, the Colton family's business, was publicly traded, but the majority of the shares were still held by a core group in the Seattle area, the family and some investors who'd been around longer than Alex had. George Tarkinson wasn't just a shareholder, he was a friend of the Coltons, and he'd known Nick forever. But Nick hadn't even found time to have dinner with his family, so it seemed unlikely he'd want to reach out to family friends if his motivation was purely social. "What the hell is he up to?" Alex mused.

"Blake hasn't told you anything? You're the lawyer, right? If he was planning something, you'd be involved?"

"Well… I'm on retainer, but I'm not in-house counsel. If Blake wanted to use someone else, he'd certainly be within his rights. But…" How much to say? "I don't know anything, George. But keep me in the loop, will you? I'm not on the board, and I don't own enough shares to get an invite of my own, I don't think—at least, Nick hasn't called me yet." Those words shouldn't have brought mixed emotions, a combination of anticipation and dread and disappointment, but they did. Nick hadn't called Alex. He'd been in town for almost a full day, and hadn't bothered to pick up the phone and contact his oldest friend. But Alex wasn't a little boy anymore, waiting around to be blessed with Nick's golden presence. "Did he leave a number where you could reach him? I'd like to look into this."

There was a pause, and Alex realized that George was surprised Alex didn't already have Nick's contact information, and maybe wondering whether it was appropriate for him to share it. But after a couple of seconds he said, "Yeah, sure, hang on," and then read out a number starting with a New York area code.

"Thanks, George," Alex said, and hung up. He looked at the paper where he'd scribbled the phone number. Nick Colton. After all these years, he was only a few digits away. But Alex hesitated. Maybe he should call Blake first, before bumbling into some secret that could be family business. But there was no way. Blake was too preoccupied with his daughter and hopes of reconciliation with his prodigal son; he didn't have energy left over for a bold business move, and he certainly wouldn't have carried on the charade that he and Nick were barely in touch.

No; whatever Nick was up to, Blake had no idea about it. And that was enough to help Alex make up his mind. Blake was vulnerable, and he needed to be protected. And Nick… well, Nick needed to stop being a secretive asshole. Alex punched the numbers into his phone decisively, and when he heard Nick's cautious greeting he said, "Hi. It's Alex. We need to talk."

CHAPTER THREE

Nick liked the bar at the Four Seasons. Clean, modern lines, but warm colors to keep it from feeling too impersonal. And lots of beautiful people to watch. Ordinarily he would have felt right at home, but just then he was far from relaxed. He wondered if he should add a mid-day massage to his regimen, then smiled at his idiocy. It didn't matter if he was tense in the middle of the day. It was good, probably; it would make him sharper, more alert. As long as he could get enough sleep at night, tension wasn't a problem.

Besides, this was surely the last of the nerve-wracking meetings. He'd already dealt with his father and the new wife. Now Alex, and after that, just business. Business was exciting, but not anxiety-producing. It would all be fine.

Then Nick glanced across the bar and saw Alex. His thoughts skidded sideways, became emotions, and ricocheted around his head before escaping and flooding his entire body. Alex. Older, a man rather than a boy, but still lean and beautiful, his warm skin begging to be touched, his deep brown eyes ready to dance in shared joy or cry with sympathy. God, he was maybe even better looking, a little more weight making his delicate features more masculine. Alex.

He saw Nick and his luscious mouth curved into a tentative smile. Nick forced his body into motion, pulling himself up from his chair and waiting for Alex to make his way across the room. He extended his hand at the appropriate time and was strangely conscious of his grip, making sure it was neither too tight nor too loose as he shook Alex's warm, familiar hand and said, "Alex. Good to see you again," in the most casual tone he could muster.

"Good to see you, too," Alex replied, but his eyes were wary. "It's been too long."

"Yeah, a long time," Nick agreed noncommittally. *Had* it been too long? He was beginning to worry that it hadn't been quite long enough. He distracted himself by nodding the server over, and tried to collect himself while she took care of Alex's drink order. Alex was just another guy. An old friend, sure. An old lover. That was no big deal. He just had to keep himself from remembering that Alex was the only man he'd ever loved, and the only one who'd ever broken his heart.

There was an awkward silence when the server left. Alex was the one to break it, saying, "I do a lot of work for your father. Law. I'm a lawyer."

"Yeah, I read that. Congratulations—you used to talk about going to law school." And then, because sometimes it was easier to be annoying than to be vulnerable, Nick added, "I remember you being interested in public-interest stuff, though. You were going to be a crusader for justice. You ended up doing corporate work?"

Alex shifted in his chair, obviously happy to let the server distract him as she set a beer in front of him. "Yeah. It pays a lot better."

"And you can still do pro bono stuff, can't you?"

"I can. In theory. But I'm a junior associate. Right now I'm working pretty hard on making money for the firm."

"So you don't actually do any charitable stuff?"

"I've done a little. But no, not as much as I'd like."

"Oh." Nick let just a little judgment bleed into his tone. He didn't actually care whether Alex was a greedy corporate shill, but he was pretty sure Alex would feel bad about it. And making Alex feel bad felt good. He'd rejected Nick when Nick wasn't good enough for him? Well, maybe Alex wasn't quite the paragon of virtue he considered himself after all. Nick smiled forgivingly. "Well, maybe someday, right?"

"I hope so." Alex shifted in his chair. "Look, Nick…" And then he didn't say anything.

"I'm looking. What do you want me to see?" Then, just because he could, Nick let his eyes run down Alex's conservatively suited body as far as he could until the table got in the way, and then slowly back to Alex's face. Which wasn't looking especially pleased with the way the conversation was going.

"What are you doing in Seattle, Nick?"

"Business. And getting tested for that bone-marrow thing."

"What kind of business?" Damn, Alex was really hot when he frowned.

"In what capacity are you asking, Mr. Junior Associate? Trying to drum up a few more billable hours?"

"I'm asking as a friend of your father's. And, yeah, as his lawyer, too."

In Nick's daydreams, this scene had been between him and his father, but there was a certain satisfaction in playing it out with Alex. Maybe this was even better. Blake had hurt Nick, but not the same way Alex had. Nick had always known his father was disappointed in him, had always known better than to rely on Blake. But Alex—Nick had trusted Alex completely, right up until that final moment.

"I've made a lot of money since you last saw me. I got lucky and picked up a job as an assistant to an entrepreneur. I learned a lot. Enough to build up a bit of a stake with a variety of small deals, then added to it when I got access to my trust fund. It all grew from there; if you know what you're doing, there's a lot of money to be made while people are losing their shirts. The last couple years, I've been focusing on being an activist shareholder. I buy a stake in companies that aren't being run properly, then make an offer to take them over. I buy up some more stock when people bail out during the transition, and then I install my own people and turn the company around. I make it profitable again."

"It's that easy? You don't need any specific industry knowledge, you can just magically fix any ailing company?"

"You'd be surprised by what a difference good, attentive management can make. But you'd also be surprised by how locked in some people are to the industry they *think* they're in. As far as I'm concerned, all corporations are in the moneymaking industry, period. And yes, I have specific knowledge of that."

It wasn't clear how much Alex understood about Nick's plans, but it was obvious he didn't like them. "You're planning to do this to SeaCo? Your father's preoccupied with a daughter who may be terminally ill, and you're planning to steal his company away from him?"

"I'm doing what I can to help with the sick daughter. The rest of it… I'm not *stealing* anything. If he likes what I'm doing, he can keep his shares; if he doesn't, he can sell them to me at a reasonable price. There's no theft involved."

"But when you talk about installing your own people, you're talking about kicking him out as CEO."

"He's been taking a dollar a year in salary since the economy tanked, and he's not pulling in anything in the way of dividends or bonuses, either. I'm going to relieve him of the burden of spending seventy hours a week at a job that makes him no money. A job he's no longer good at."

"He's only having trouble because he's worried about his daughter!"

"No. Profits have been declining for almost a decade. It's because he's not keeping up with the times. Handcrafted toys? That's the signature line? And even the mass-produced stuff is way too expensive for what it is. Modern kids want electronics, not dump trucks so well-made they'll survive generations of abuse." Nick raised his hands. "But I'm getting ahead of myself. Those are my assumptions, borne out by preliminary research, but I'll let the team work out the details. The important thing is comparing earnings to assets, and SeaCo is not doing well in that area. It should be doing better."

"He's been having trouble for almost a decade?" Alex sounded bitter now. His brown eyes were angry, and Nick found the sight surprisingly unpleasant. "Can you think of anything else that's been wrong in Blake's life for the last ten or so years? Maybe it's hard for him to do a great job at work when he's completely lost contact with the son he was planning to hand the company over to."

"Give me a break, Alex. You really think he was going to let me anywhere *near* that company? He'd barely let me drive his car.

More likely he got distracted by the hot young wife and the adorable tots. Or maybe he's not distracted at all. Maybe he's just not good enough. The reasons don't matter; the results do. And his results have been brutal." Nick shrugged with deliberate disdain. He wouldn't let himself soften. He'd been looking forward to this, working toward this, for years. He wasn't going to be distracted by sentiment, or by the fascinating strength he could see in Alex's hands as they formed into fists on the table. "The company's sitting on some prime assets, and it's time they were used more efficiently."

"Blake always says the *employees* are the company's biggest assets." Alex raised an eyebrow as he waited for a response.

"That's insane. The employees are the biggest *liability*. The salaries and benefits are way too generous for what they're producing, and the pension plan? It was almost a deal-breaker. But we've figured out ways to work around that."

"Figured out ways to work around the pension?" Alex sounded incredulous. "What does that mean, exactly?"

"We'd use a variety of tools: cutting back on future benefits, allowing employees to withdraw from their pension accounts to cover current expenses. Definitely moving away from a defined benefits plan. Whatever it takes to get the company *making* money instead of losing it." Nick let himself sit back in his chair and take a sip of his drink. "I think it's something the shareholders are going to be very interested in."

"So this is your plan. This is why you're here." Nick refused to let himself be upset by the disgust in Alex's voice. "After all these years, all of us waiting for you, wishing you'd come back—"

"Wait a second." There were things Nick could ignore, and things he couldn't. "Just how much revisionist history have you been writing? You were all sitting around waiting for me? Really? Dad started a whole new family, for Christ's sake, and I forgot to say it earlier, but congratulations on your *engagement*. And you were the ones who wanted me to leave in the first place! Now I've made myself into the person you all wanted me to be: someone responsible and ambitious, goal-oriented and serious… and *that's* a problem, too?" Nick huffed out a disbelieving breath. "And you wonder why I stayed away? You're impossible to please!"

But Alex wasn't intimidated, not by Nick or by the attention they were starting to draw from other tables. "Does everything always have to be an extreme with you? Back then, you couldn't goof off a little, or have a *little* fun; you had to go completely overboard. A night out wasn't complete unless the cops were involved. And then you couldn't just back off a little and give me some space, you had to disappear entirely for over ten years!" Alex's expression of amazement was almost comical. "Now, you can't have a regular job like everybody else; you've turned yourself into a fucking corporate raider. Jesus, Nick, get some therapy! Bipolar disorder can be inherited, you know."

Nick felt his features freeze and could see the anger fade from Alex's face as he noticed. References to Nick's mother, her illness and her death... Alex knew better. At least, the old Alex had. Nick fished his wallet out of his jacket pocket and tucked a couple of twenties under his glass. "So I'll be continuing my meetings with the board members and other interested shareholders. If your client would like to see our proposal, he can contact my lawyer to set something up." Nick pulled a business card from his wallet and dropped it halfway across the table. "I'll be making a motion at the AGM, and based on what I've seen so far, I'll be successful. If the current board won't agree with my plans, I'll use the votes to install my own slate of board members." That was all he needed to say. He stood up and Alex was out of his seat at almost the same moment.

"I'm sorry," he said. "That was a tasteless thing to say, and I know... well. I shouldn't have said that. I apologize."

There had been a time when Nick would have forgiven Alex anything. But that time was long gone. "I expect I'll see you at the AGM. Say hi to your family for me." He was heading for the door before Alex could raise his arm for a handshake, and he kept moving, walking briskly out of the lounge and through the lobby, out the main doors and down the street. He didn't have a destination in mind, but that wasn't important. He just had to keep moving. It had been a good strategy for him so far, and he saw no reason to give it up.

Alex sank back into the upholstered chair and replayed his words in his mind. Jesus. He reached for his beer, then changed his mind and stretched across to grab Nick's apparently untouched glass. It looked like scotch, and Alex wanted something a bit stronger to burn the taste of his own cruelty from his mouth.

He took a sip and almost spat it out, then rolled it carefully over his tongue to make sure he was tasting it correctly. Iced tea. Nick Colton, who in his teens had actually poured beer on his Wheaties several times just so he could call it the breakfast of champions, was drinking iced tea at four in the afternoon. In a bar. Alex didn't know Nick at all anymore. And the one thing he *had* known had been a reference to the most painful event of Nick's life.

He started to reach for his beer, then abandoned it and slumped back in his chair. He'd been an idiot. He'd been so high on the idea that Nick was looking for something more, trying to reconcile with his family… trying to reconcile with Alex himself. He felt a churning in his gut as he realized that he had, indeed, hoped that Nick had come home for *him*.

It was insane. He was happily engaged. Maybe he'd just wanted their friendship back; he'd never found anyone else with whom he'd had the same easy rapport, the same unspoken understanding. The same passion. God damn it, he'd wanted the passion, as much as any of the rest of it.

Alex had never been with a man other than Nick. He'd concentrated on his studies for a few years after Nick left, and then he'd gone to law school and met Marta, and they'd gotten along so well. He wanted a family, and so did she. It wasn't a grand, romantic affair, but it was a good partnership. It was safe, and it had made Alex's family very happy.

Nick wasn't an option anyway, he reminded himself, so there was no point in obsessing over it. Especially not when there was so much else he needed to be doing. Starting with a phone call he really didn't want to make.

He went out to the lobby, found a secluded corner, and pulled out his cell.

Blake sounded tired when he answered, and Alex didn't want to add to the man's burdens, but there was no way around it. "I just had drinks with Nick," he said. "I don't know how to say this, Blake, but…"

"He's not backing out of the testing, is he?"

"No! No, that's still fine, as far as I know. It's a business issue."

"Business." Alex could picture Blake trying to collect his thoughts. "Nick?"

"Apparently." Alex decided to dive right in. "He calls it activist shareholding, but I think you and I would call it corporate raiding. He's set his sights on SeaCo Toys."

There was a long pause. "Wait. He wants—he's staging a hostile takeover of SeaCo?"

"I need to check a few definitions to see if it would actually be classified that way, but in essence, yes."

"That makes no sense. It's… is it because of the kids? Because he doesn't want to share the company with them?"

Alex hadn't thought of that possibility, and he quickly considered it before saying, "I'm not sure. Maybe. But I didn't really get that feeling. He didn't seem too interested in them one way or the other. I think… Well, really, I have no idea. I thought I'd still know him, once we got together. Thought we'd still have things in common. Still be friends. But he was like a total stranger."

Blake's voice was quiet. "I'm sorry, Alex. I know you were hoping for something more."

Alex wanted to stay focused on business. "I assume you want to fight the takeover? Or at least for me to look into it? I didn't get a detailed view of the changes he has in mind, but he did mention that he'd found a way around the pension plan. It sounds like he wants to make some significant changes."

"That sounds troubling. I don't know. I need to *talk* to him. He's being so distant; I don't know how to reach him." Blake sighed. "I guess I never did. Anna and Damon are so much easier. Nick was always… well, I guess he was always his mother's son. He looks like me, but that's all. They were so close. Maybe because I spent so much time at work." Another sigh. "It's fitting, I suppose. I neglected my relationship with my son in order to build my company, and now that same son is coming to take the company away. So I'll be left with nothing."

"Even if it came to that, you'd still have a beautiful wife and two lovely children."

"Nothing to show for the first forty-five years of my life, though."

"You'd be financially stable. You have enough stock in the company for that. He can't take the stock away; he'll have to buy it. And only if you want to sell." It felt strange to be giving a pep talk to his mentor, but Alex pressed on. "And it's far from guaranteed that Nick will win. You still have about 30% of the stock, and we know who holds another 45 to 50%, I'd say. So the *most* he could have is 25%. He can't force a change in management without the support of several other shareholders. I say we fight it."

"The company *hasn't* been doing well, Alex." Blake sounded old, his self-doubt making his voice weak. "Maybe it's time for a change. Maybe the shareholders will agree with him, and want someone else to take over."

"We're in the middle of a global recession. And you've always had the shareholders' support. They've understood what you're doing with the company, and they've approved. There's no reason to think they'll abandon ship now."

"No reason but Nick. Some of them know him. Maybe they'll see it as a natural changing of the guard."

"They know him from *ten years ago*, Blake. They know him as an irresponsible hell-raiser, not a corporate leader. I think familiarity will work against him, in this case."

"Is he good at this, Alex? Can he actually turn the thing

around, make it profitable again?"

"I don't know. He seems pretty confident. He talks like financing isn't an issue, which suggests that he's made some money for himself along the way. That's all I know right now, but I'd really like to get some people on it and find out more."

"If he had come to me, if he'd asked for a place in the company, I'd have been thrilled."

"I don't think he wanted to have it given to him. I think he wants to take it." Alex needed to get Blake back in gear, keep him from wallowing in pointless regrets. "There's a dinner meeting tonight. Seven o'clock at *Delilah's*." It was a gamble, but it might pay off. "I think we should be there. We're both shareholders. We should hear what he's planning."

"You want us to crash his dinner party?"

"Why not? The old Nick would have thought it was hilarious."

"I don't think we're dealing with the old Nick anymore, Alex."

That was hard to argue with. "Fine. But we should still crash his party. Because he's sure as hell planning to crash yours."

CHAPTER FOUR

Nick felt electrified, in the best possible way. He felt like he was somehow more *alive* than normal—more intense, more present. It was the same way he always felt when he pushed just a little beyond what other people thought was possible. He beamed as he shook the hand of the most recent arrival, and his expression was absolutely genuine. He was high on adrenaline.

His good mood faltered a little when he remembered Alex's dig about bipolar disorder; the smug bastard would probably classify this as a manic episode. But he'd be wrong. Nick had been on guard against his mother's illness all his life, and he knew the difference between mania and legitimate excitement. His current joy was brought on by all the positive, exciting things that were happening in Nick's environment, not by an imbalance in his brain. He was fine, and Alex was an asshole.

"George, good to see you!" he said with another wide smile, drawing the newcomer further into the private dining room. "I'd like to introduce you to some of my team: this is Andrea Dean, my lawyer, and Scott Bishop handles our finances. Greg Asano's our general go-to guy. And this is Colin Philson—he's done great work in the past, turning companies around and getting them started in a new direction, and I think he might be an excellent match for SeaCo Toys."

The team moved in on George like smiling, chatting piranhas, and Nick let himself step back and survey the room. Everything was going well. The atmosphere was friendly but professional, the right people were talking to each other, and the table was almost full. Everyone had come. Everyone except…

Motion in the doorway caught his attention, and he felt his excitement ramp up just a little bit more. They'd done it. They'd come. He could feel when the rest of the room noticed them, and he stepped forward with a big smile and a hand outstretched for shaking. "Dad. Alex. Good to see you. I was starting to worry that you might not make it."

Alex was realizing that he was in way over his head. Blake Colton was *his* client, and Alex hadn't wanted to let the firm's partners get their claws into him. He'd asked for some research help, because he couldn't get everything done in the couple of hours between the afternoon meeting and the dinner, but he'd wanted to make sure he was still the one in charge. So he'd set the strategy, and Blake had taken his advice... and now the wide smile on Nick's face made it crystal clear that they'd blundered into some sort of trap.

"We were just going to sit down. I saved you seats together." Nick waved toward the table and Alex saw two place settings, complete with glossy booklets clearly labeled with Alex and Blake's names. Nick turned to the group. "Alex doesn't have all that many shares in the company, but he's an old friend of the family, so I wanted to include him. I hope that's okay with everyone."

"You're the one paying," one of the board members said with a laugh, and the others joined in. Seven men, three women, their faces familiar to Alex from countless meetings over the years—and four strangers, looking as polished and attentive as Nick. The man had brought a team of clones with him from New York.

"Come sit down," Nick said with a smile. The aggressive tension from that afternoon was gone, replaced by relaxed congeniality. There was a distance, certainly; Nick was acting as if they were acquaintances, not family and an old friend. Old lover. But his happiness seemed completely genuine. The old Nick's emotions had been simple and straightforward, his actions completely transparent to Alex. This Nick? He was something else, something considerably more complex.

Alex was ready to head obediently to his seat, but while Blake might have shown his vulnerability to Alex earlier, when it came to business he was accustomed to being in charge. He paused just long enough for the attention of the room to shift to him, then said, "This was a lovely idea, Nick." Blake Colton, CEO, smiled at his audience. "We've spent so much time together, over the years, but it's almost always focused on business. We never seem to stop and enjoy each other's company." He clapped Nick on the shoulder but kept his face turned toward the crowd. "But you all remember Nick well enough to know that he's not one to pass up an opportunity for a night out on the town!"

The shareholders laughed good-naturedly, but the point was made. Alex snuck a peek at Nick, almost afraid to see the familiar signs of his friend trying to conceal hurt feelings. Instead, Nick looked happy that Blake was fighting back. "Absolutely," Nick said easily. "I may not be as irresponsible as I was when I was a kid, but I still enjoy seeing old friends, especially when they bring new ideas. I've been really impressed by some of the creative suggestions I've been hearing over the last couple days, and I look forward to us all discussing them this evening. It's a shame you didn't get together and share them earlier!" He shook his head with slightly exaggerated regret. "I'm trying not to think about the lost opportunities over the years, if you've all had such great ideas all along, just waiting for someone to ask." He returned his father's shoulder clap and smiled again. "Please, sit down," he said in a quiet but still friendly voice. "We'll enjoy the meal, and then I hope it won't ruin the evening if we do a little business afterward."

This time Blake complied, and Alex trailed after him like a well-trained puppy. He felt a sudden flash of envy for Nick. He'd cut all ties, done things his own way, and now he was back, triumphant and powerful. Alex had followed every rule he could find or imagine, had been respectful and compliant, and what the hell had it gotten him? He was a slave to billable hours, still dependent on the patronage of the man who'd been looking after him his whole life, and somehow engaged to get married to... Wait. He was engaged to marry a lovely woman. She cared about him, and he cared about her. They would be good partners, and good parents. That wasn't something for him to feel dissatisfied over.

He snuck one more look at Nick, seated at the head of the table and chatting happily to the elderly woman beside him. Mrs. Dorothy Cavanaugh held about 8% of the company's stock, and she looked absolutely charmed by Nick. And who wouldn't be, Alex thought. Nick had been almost too pretty as a boy, his fair hair and deep-blue eyes making him look a little fragile. He'd masked that as a teen with shaggy, unkempt locks and sloppy clothes, but it had still been apparent at times. When he was naked, his rough curls smoothed away from his face, his gaze locked on Alex's... he'd been so beautiful it had been hard for Alex to breathe. Now, though, he'd filled out, and his skin had a tan that couldn't have come from either Seattle *or* New York this early in the year. His hair was short, his clothes were impeccable, and he looked absolutely masculine. And still absolutely desirable.

Damn it! Alex needed to stop thinking like that.

"You're still at Brown, Borden and Clark?" the man sitting next to him asked, and Alex had to take a moment to collect himself and remember the name of his firm.

"I am," he said. "And you've had a great quarter at the bank, I understand." He needed to focus on this and keep his mind off Nick Colton. Getting distracted was bad for business, and not too good for Alex's peace of mind, either.

The dinner passed quickly. Nick's energy simmered down but didn't boil away, and by the time the dessert was cleared and after-dinner drinks were served, he felt like a runner who'd found his stride. When the rhythm of the conversation slowed, he let his guests' attention flow to him and then waited for silence.

"Thank you all for coming this evening. I know we'll be together again in a few days at the Annual General Meeting, but I wanted to take this opportunity to put some ideas in front of you so you'll have time to think them over and make the decision that's best for the company, but also the decision that's best for you, and for your families." That was his trump card, he'd decided. These people might have enough personal loyalty to tolerate his father's incompetence if it were only their own bank accounts being affected, but if he could help them see that their inaction was hurting their children's futures, they'd have to act.

He had a speech, carefully prepared to sound extemporaneous, and he gave it with as much charisma as he could muster. He was suggesting a change in leadership, and a change in direction. It wasn't a personal decision; it was based on business needs. It was great that the company had such a strong sense of tradition, but the world was changing and the economy was getting worse every day; emotion was great for families (he smiled warmly somewhere in the direction of Blake's shoulder) but it had no place in business decisions. He had some ideas for the company, as laid out in the packages he'd left at each person's plate, but he was also really excited to hear other people's suggestions.

There was an appreciative buzz when he sat down. He waited for his father's rebuttal, but nothing came. He needed to play it cool, but he managed to glance over casually, and he saw his father watching him, his face calm and thoughtful. Evaluating in just the same way he'd done when Nick was a child, still making desperate bids for positive attention rather than carelessly accepting the negative reactions. The familiar gaze combined with the memories made Nick's skin crawl. Instinctively, as he had when he was a boy, he turned to Alex for comfort.

And just as when they were boys, Alex was there. He didn't understand what Nick needed, maybe, but his forehead creased in a concerned frown and he returned Nick's gaze with an open expression. By then Nick had recovered, though. It had been stupid, a half-second twinge of memory. He was an adult, and he'd worked hard to get away from that childishness. He was fine. He looked around the room and saw that everyone was happy, drinking and chatting, and he decided it was time for a quick break.

He made his way through the restaurant to the bathroom, which was empty and quiet. He was washing his hands when the door swished open behind him. Nick watched in the mirror as Alex stepped tentatively into the ornately furnished room. His gaze found Nick's and he said, "You okay? You seemed a bit weird there for a second."

"Only for a second?" Nick turned the water off and dried his hands on one of the waiting towels, then eased around to face Alex. "That's not bad. There've been times when I've seemed a bit weird for days on end."

But Alex didn't bite. He stepped a little closer, still watching Nick closely. "You sure you want to do this? I have no idea what Blake's thinking, but... you don't want to try to be a family again? He's fighting back, now, but that's because you took him by surprise. He was so excited when he heard you were coming back. Maybe you could give him a chance. Keep it light at first, if you want, but—"

It was the sincere concern in Alex's tone that did it, Nick decided later. That and the way Alex's long eyelashes brushed his cheeks, the gentle curve of his lips as he spoke. And, of course, the ever-attractive outrageousness of the idea. He stepped forward, Alex stepped back instinctively and ran into the wall beside the door, and Nick moved in the rest of the way. A brief pause, enough time for Alex to object if he really wanted to, and then Nick's hand was on the back of Alex's head, pulling him forward until their lips met.

It wasn't a hard kiss. It was sweet, Nick's lips soft as he felt Alex stiffen in surprised resistance without moving away. Nick's fingers gently ruffled Alex's hair, and his other hand found Alex's hip—not a crude grab, but gentle contact. When Alex relaxed, Nick leaned back just enough to break the kiss. He stood there and enjoyed the view as Alex reacted, his eyes widening, his pupils expanding, and that beautiful flush creeping over his brown cheeks.

Nick smiled, and when he leaned in again Alex's lips opened to meet him. It was so familiar yet so different, and Nick wanted to spend some time exploring this. He wanted to learn Alex's new taste, learn the body of the man instead of the boy. But he still had enough instinct for self-preservation to make himself pull away.

He took one last look at Alex's kiss-softened face and smiled softly. "It's good to see you again, Alex." It really was. But that wasn't why he was in town. "And it looks like I'm going to be around a while longer, so maybe I can meet your fiancée, too. I'm sure she's really great."

Alex blinked once. Twice. Then he shoved Nick away and

stood with his fists clenched, staring at Nick in disbelief. "You're a son of a bitch."

"Yeah," Nick agreed quietly, and he eased past Alex and headed back to the party.

CHAPTER FIVE

The dinner was breaking up by the time Alex made it back out to the dining room. Nick was operating smoothly, speaking to each departing guest, joking with them like they were all old friends. Blake, on the other hand, seemed withdrawn. Not sullen, and certainly not intimidated, just remote. He looked as if the scene were a play being put on for his entertainment, but he wasn't sure he was pleased with the quality of the actors.

Alex tried to focus on that. Blake had changed a lot since Nick left, he realized. He'd been determined to be a better father to his new family, and the effort had softened him. When he'd heard Nick was returning he'd been full of hope, and had clearly wanted a reconciliation. But the man Alex was looking at right now was the old Blake, the calm, remote businessman who regarded his son as a problem to be solved. There was no emotion here, not even intellect: just cunning. But how was he applying that craftiness; what was he planning?

And what about Nick? Jesus, what about Nick? His strong hand on the back of Alex's neck, his lips soft and confident, his body...

"You feeling okay?" George Tarkinson was at Alex's elbow, looking at him with concern. "I just asked you two times if you know what Blake's going to do about this."

"Oh. Sorry. I was thinking. Trying to figure it all out." That was more true than Alex wanted to admit. "No, I'm not sure if Blake's made a decision yet. You know him, though—he's always got a plan. He'll just wait for the right time, I expect."

"I'm thinking about voting for the change," George blurted out, and then looked relieved to have said it. "Blake's a good man, and he's done a good job with the company for a long time. But Nick's right—we haven't been getting the results we used to, and it's not just the economy. A lot of the ideas in that business plan... they're good ideas, Alex. They're things Blake should have done years ago."

"Well, maybe we should think of this as Nick having given us a bit of free consulting." Alex hoped his smile seemed sincere. "There's no reason we can't act on some or all of the suggestions he's made, without going so far as to change leadership. Any shareholder can give us ideas, and he's given us some. That's all this has to be."

"Will Blake take them? He and Nick don't seem too close these days. Not that they ever really were, that I saw."

"They're still family." Alex wished he felt as confident as he sounded. "And they're both shareholders. It's in their mutual interests to help the company make money. I'm sure Blake will be happy to consult with Nick, just like he'd be happy to consult with anyone else."

"And would Nick consult with Blake?" George's eyes were shrewd, and Alex was glad he didn't have to try to lie to the man.

"I'm not sure. I can't really figure out what Nick's up to, to be honest. I mean, like I said, he's a shareholder, and he wants the company to be profitable." This was good. Alex knew what he needed to say, and he was able to focus on George and ignore everyone else, including Nick. "He's been gone for a long time. I'm still looking into just what he was up to while he was away, but we know he hasn't stayed anywhere too long. He hasn't built anything the way Blake built up SeaCo Toys. If Nick is interested in the business, I'm sure Blake would be happy to show him the ropes. But really, doesn't it seem a bit weird that Nick's interested in coming back to the company all of a sudden, after so long with no interest?"

Nick's voice came from right behind Alex. "That's the second time you've called me 'weird' in the last fifteen minutes," he said, good-naturedly draping his arm around Alex's neck. Its weight was distracting, and the warmth bled through Alex's cotton shirt into his over-sensitized skin. Things got even worse when Nick leaned in closer and murmured, "You remember what happened last time you said it, don't you?"

Alex forced himself to laugh as he jerked away. "Yeah; it wasn't too pleasant." He needed to get out of there, but he wanted to be sure he was the one who left the last word echoing through George's brain. "Thanks for dinner, Nick. Always good to see you. George, are you parked across the street? I can walk over with you…"

"Valet," George said. Of course. Alex should have known that. But George was saying his goodbyes and moving toward the exit anyway, so Alex decided to count it as a victory. He raised a hand to Blake with a questioning look. Was he needed, or did Blake have a plan of his own? Blake nodded in dismissal, so Alex kept moving. He followed George outside and made small talk while they waited for George's car to be retrieved, and then he jogged across the busy street to the parking garage.

He was up the stairs and into the parking area when it all hit him. He'd just kissed a man. Nick. He'd kissed Nick Colton. The first time, maybe he could pretend Nick had kissed him and he'd been too surprised to resist, but after Nick moved away and then came back? Alex had kissed him—and he'd wanted more. God only knew how much further he'd have gone, there in a public bathroom, if Nick hadn't put a stop to it.

Alex bent over and braced his hands on his knees. He tried to take deep breaths, but each inhalation reminded him of the scent of Nick's aftershave. Nick Colton. Back in town, back in Alex's life… and making things just as crazy as he always had.

Nick had expected that his father would stick around for a conversation after everyone else left, and he wasn't disappointed.

"Brandy?" Blake asked, his eyes flickering to the server just long enough to let her know she was needed.

"Sure." Nick didn't drink any more, but he could hold a snifter if he wanted to. "Do you want to go into the bar? I think they have easy chairs in there, and I expect the staff would like to get this room cleared up."

"For what you must have paid for that little shindig, the staff can wait." Blake settled back into the chair he'd had during dinner. Nick could feel the power games beginning. Not only had Blake chosen this room, now he'd chosen the position at the table. Nick could resist, but not gracefully. And it didn't matter too much, anyway. He had the *real* power here, so Blake's maneuvering was mostly for show.

But, just to make the game interesting, Nick selected a chair one away from Blake's and pulled it a couple feet back from the table before he sat down. He wasn't out in the middle of the aisle, but he was far enough to the side that Blake would either have to turn his own chair or crane his neck awkwardly to make eye contact. The older man turned his chair, and Nick awarded himself a point.

"Two brandies, please," Blake said to the attentive server. A point to him for taking charge of their order, except…

"Actually, make mine a cognac, please," Nick said. "I saw Hennessy XO on your list, didn't I?" He raised an eyebrow at Blake. "I'm still paying—you sure you don't want the good stuff?" Nick was pretty sure he deserved two points for that: one for changing the order, the other for implying that Blake couldn't afford to buy fine brandy on his own.

But Blake didn't seem ruffled. "No, I'm fine," he said, and as the server walked away he added, "It's not like this is a special occasion. Just another business dinner."

"Might not be too many more. Have you thought about what you'll do after the vote? Obviously we'll need a transition plan, but we can probably have you ready to go in a couple months. Do you think you'll do a full retirement, or do you have some other projects in mind?"

"You're counting your votes before they hatch, son." Blake gave Nick another long, thoughtful look. "Why are you doing this? I don't understand your interest in SeaCo. Lord knows you were never interested in it *before* you left town."

"It's a troubled company with a lot of assets. It's trading well below value. It's perfectly suited to a move like this. Really, you should be surprised someone else hasn't done something about it already. Of course, I've been having friends and colleagues buy up available stock at a pretty steady rate for the past few years. After a few private deals last week, I own about 22% of the company. The paperwork's been filed."

Blake nodded. "We wondered about that. Our stock price seemed artificially high compared to our earnings, but we couldn't figure out why."

"I was doing you favors even before I came back to town."

"Let's not talk about this in terms of doing favors," Blake said, and for the first time there was a trace of irritation in his voice. Interesting. They broke the conversation as the server placed a snifter on the table near each of them. She seemed a bit unclear how to handle Nick's chair placement, but he nodded his approval at her choice. It wasn't like he was going to be drinking the stuff.

The server left, and Nick smiled at his father. "You don't think I'm doing you a favor? I mean, you've been taking a dollar a year in salary for how long? How long can you live with no income from your primary business? Hell, most of the stock I've been buying up has probably been yours, sold to make ends meet."

"No," Blake said calmly. "I've sold some other assets, but not the company stock. It's a family company, and the stock is for my kids."

That stung, thinking of the two little strangers inheriting it all, but Nick just smiled. "You think they're going to enjoy owning a shitload of stock in a bankrupt company? Would have been wiser to sell the SeaCo and build them a portfolio of healthier investments."

"Is that what you'd like me to do with your share?" Blake's voice was quiet but his gaze was intent, watching for Nick's reaction.

"I… sorry, I didn't know you were including me in the 'kid' category." It was something to say while his brain sorted through it.

Blake frowned at him. "I never disowned you, Nick. I never even asked you to move out, and I certainly didn't ask you to leave town and cut off contact for a damned decade." He leaned forward. "Your extended tantrum had nothing to do with me; you left because things weren't going well between you and Alex. Let's not pretend we both don't know that."

"Nothing to do with your decision to throw me under the bus in order to rescue Alex?" Nick fought to keep his expression calm and pleasant. "But there's no point to rehashing all that; I don't see how any of it is relevant to the current situation."

"It's relevant to what's happening between you and Alex. And something did happen tonight. I don't know what, and I don't want to. But he's not as good as you are at hiding things; he never has been. So I know *something* happened, and it upset him. I don't like to see that. He's worked his ass off, and he's come a long way. He's in a good place, and he doesn't deserve to have that destroyed as part of some stupid game you're playing."

It was surprising how easy it was to fall back into old patterns. "It's good to see things haven't changed around here—you're still protecting poor little Alex against the depravity of your evil son." When you don't have anything productive to say, fall back on bitterness and resentment: that was Nick's motto.

"I never said you were evil, Nick, and I never thought it, either. But you were always thoughtless. And just because you've put on this veneer of being a planner, aware of every nuance of a business situation… nice touch with the personalized packages waiting for us tonight, by the way… just because you're doing better on the surface, it doesn't prove you've grown even a little bit in terms of pulling your head out of your ass and thinking about the people you claim to care about."

"Who are these people I 'claim to care about,' exactly? What the hell do you know about that?" Nick was done with this conversation: time to kill it. "And what do you know about the people *you* claim to care about? Alex is your golden boy, but only because *he* allows you to make him over in your image. That sweet little kid who dreamed about doing public-interest law, fighting to help the disadvantaged? You turned him into a corporate fucking lawyer! The teenager who somehow found the courage to come out to his conservative Catholic family is now magically engaged to a woman!" Nick stood up, but didn't move away. Instead, he leaned down, hovering over his father and staring him in the eye. "I don't know how Alex feels about corporate law. From what I've heard, he's solid, but not exactly a superstar. I think he's smart enough to be a *great* lawyer if his heart was in it, so I suspect the answer is he's not too inspired. I can't say for sure about that." And now for the best part. He smiled wolfishly and said, "But I *can* say, for sure, that he's not nearly as straight as he seems to have fooled you all into believing. I can tell you how hot he was in the bathroom, how he practically melted as soon as I touched him." Nick leaned back, but kept his smile. "I can tell you how he came after me, begging for more."

"Don't do that, Nick." Blake wasn't exactly pleading, but there was an unusual tone to his voice that Nick would have liked to record for further analysis. "If you're angry, you're angry with me. Don't drag Alex into it."

"Wait a second... I thought *you* didn't do anything wrong. I thought the only reason I left town was because things weren't going well between me and Alex. You changing your mind on that?"

"A boy breaking up with you over a decade ago does *not* excuse you trying to ruin his life today."

"Ruin his life? Ruin his web of lies, his careful disguises that he thinks he has to wear so you all will accept him and be proud of him?" Nick shook his head. He knew it was hypocritical to pretend his motives were noble, but he'd think about that later. For now, he drew himself up to his full height and said, "Maybe I'm trying to *save* his life. You ever think about that?"

Nick didn't really want an answer. Rather than waiting for one, he nodded with formal courtesy and headed out of the room. He'd already settled the tab with the restaurant, so he was free to ease through the gathering of late-night diners at the door and find his way out into the cool night. He hadn't arranged for a car, knowing he'd need a little decompression time after the meeting, so he started walking.

He'd been right; he had a lot to think about, questions dancing through his mind that would surely keep him awake if he couldn't address them. But he'd expected his preoccupation to be centered around business, the successes and failures of the evening. Instead, his mind kept returning to the kiss. The second one, with Alex's soft tongue meeting his, their bodies aligning from chest to thigh, the strange mix of familiarity and novelty. And more distracting than that, even, were his own words to his father. They'd been bravado, spoken in the heat of the moment, but as he thought about Alex's eager response, he wondered if maybe he hadn't stumbled upon a little bit of truth. Maybe Alex *was* trapped in a complicated charade. Maybe he *did* need Nick's help.

Nick thought about young Alex, always there to help Nick, even if the assistance was just a sympathetic ear and, later, some distracting body contact. Alex had saved Nick countless times, without a doubt. Maybe it was time for Nick to return the favor.

He doubted Alex would agree. But maybe Alex didn't really know what was best for him.

CHAPTER SIX

"Jesus Christ, Alex." Janissa sounded tired, and not just because she'd been woken from a sound sleep by her brother's panicked phone call. When Alex had arrived at her apartment, she'd taken one look at him and headed for the kitchen. He'd trailed after her and slumped over her battered oak table while she brewed a pot of herbal tea. And he'd told her the whole story, as clearly as he could manage.

She leaned back in her chair and stared at her teacup. "You're making me *really* want something stronger."

"There's none in the house, though, right?"

She smiled her appreciation of his concern and shook her head. "I'm not stupid, Alex."

But it was one more thing to think about. "If someone who used to drink a lot stops drinking—the first thought is alcoholism, right? But there must be other reasons for people to do it…"

"Is Nick not drinking anymore?" She frowned as soon as she stopped speaking. "Damn it, no! We are *not* going to turn this into a conversation about Nick Colton! We need to talk about *you*, Alex. You and Marta. She's not just your fiancée, you know. I consider her a friend, now. We hang out when you're not around. She does not deserve to get hurt by this."

"I know." Alex let his head fall back into his hands. "But how do I protect her? Do I tell her what happened and hurt her with the information, or not tell her and maybe hurt her with a lie?"

"Let's start by taking a little responsibility, okay? Let's not say 'what happened,' let's say 'what I did.' 'What happened' sounds like you weren't involved, and that's bullshit, Alex."

Janissa had never been one to suffer fools gladly, but after she became a social worker with clients in some of the city's roughest neighborhoods, she'd gotten even tougher. It wasn't always comfortable to have a conversation with her, but that was why Alex had come here. He didn't deserve to be comforted, he deserved to be yelled at. And he knew Jani would still love him afterward. "Yeah, okay. Do I tell her what I did?"

"Probably," Jani said slowly. "There's two parts to this, right? Or maybe three? There's the part where you fooled around with an old flame. That's… pretty bad, but it's also pretty common. I expect Marta would be able to get past that. If she's got half a brain, which she absolutely does, I'd expect her to give you some ground rules going forward. Like saying that you need to make sure it doesn't happen again by staying away from the source of temptation."

"It was a business meeting," Alex protested. "It's not like I went to his hotel room or something."

"You followed him to the bathroom. You fell back into the old pattern of being the one who understands him, and who has to look after him."

"I don't understand him at *all*."

"That's a conversation for another time." Janissa was a harsh taskmaster. "Part one is you fooling around with an old flame. It's workable. But, Alex, part two is that the old flame was a guy. I'm not saying Marta's homophobic, but I think she has a legitimate reason not to want to marry a gay man! Are you gay, Alex? Mami and Papi are convinced it was just a phase, another example of the insane influence Nick had on you when you were kids. You're not gay, you were just being a *really* good friend." The sarcasm in Jani's tone made her opinion pretty clear, but she kept going anyway. "I always thought that was bullshit. You're bi, at least. I've kept my mouth shut because it was nothing but a feeling. I couldn't back it up, and I didn't want to push into something that was none of my business. But given your dating history, or lack thereof… and now this… I think maybe you're truly gay, and engaged to marry someone who should just be a good friend." She sipped her tea while Alex tried to ignore her words, and then she said, "And for the record, *that* is what would hurt Marta. She deserves a husband who wants her for who she is, not because she's the socially acceptable doppelganger of the person you really want."

Alex jerked his head in surprise. "She *does* look like him! I just noticed it the other day!"

"Oh my God, Alex, you are so blind. The others are trying to ignore it, or say it's just a coincidence. And tall, blonde, blue-eyed women—they *are* a societal ideal, so maybe she's just one more example of your overachievement. But her facial structure is similar, too, with the cheekbones. And her shoulders are too broad for feminine ideals; her body type is quite masculine, even though she hides it behind frilly clothes. You really hadn't noticed any of this before?"

"Her personality is nothing like Nick's. Maybe I initially noticed her because of her looks. Maybe. But that's not what I like about her. I mean, I do like her looks. She's very attractive." Alex was digging himself into some sort of pit, here, but he wasn't quite sure how to scramble out.

"She's attractive," Jani agreed. "But are you attrac*ted*? Do you enjoy sex with her as much as you enjoyed it with Nick?"

Not a conversation Alex wanted to have with his baby sister. Not a conversation he wanted to have with anyone. "It's hard to compare. I mean, I was a kid with Nick. We were… you know… figuring things out. It was the first time—well, for me. He'd messed around a bit, with guys and girls. He taught me stuff. It was…" Alex stopped, because he absolutely refused to get hard at his sister's kitchen table. But the memories weren't easy to shut off. Sex with Nick had been fascinating; intoxicating. Alex's body had always been on fire, Nick's hands warming and cooling him simultaneously. It had been all Alex could think about when they were together, and all he longed for when they were apart. Not just the orgasms, but also the closeness, the passion. The trust.

"So, it was good," Jani said dryly, and Alex wondered how long he'd gone without speaking.

"Yes," he managed to croak.

"And with Marta?"

Alex searched for the words, then threw his hands in the air in frustration. "There's more to a relationship than scorching sex. Marta and I get along really well! We have similar values, and common goals. We both feel the same way about parenting, and that's important."

"Do you have sex at *all*?" And there was the bratty little sister, raising an eyebrow in challenge. "Because *becoming* parents is going to be a bit trickier without that…"

"Yes! Of course. Not that this is something I really want to discuss with you. But, yeah, we have sex." Not often, maybe, but that was because they were both so busy. Like Alex, Marta was a junior associate at a large downtown law firm, and she had her own set of partners to impress, her own billable hours to hoard. So it made sense that the time they spent together tended to be spent relaxing in front of the television or going over paperwork. Marta understood that Alex was from a conservative family, so she hadn't pushed him toward moving in together. And they were both so busy, it hadn't seemed important to set a date for the wedding, or to take any concrete steps toward it after the proposal. It was all completely natural.

"Are you gay, Alex?" Jani's voice was quiet, but the question was impossible to ignore.

It was also impossible to answer, at least for Alex. He stared at her mutely until she finally took pity on him and said, "Well, maybe we should talk about the third part of all this. Nick." She smiled in sympathy. "Do you think this is just about him? If Mami and Papi are right, and you were never really gay, maybe this is just a flashback to old patterns and old emotions. You can deal with it short-term by avoiding him, and then go back to the semi-happy, semi-straight boy you've been since he left the first time." She peered at him, then added, "I was wrong. There's *four* parts to this, at least. The fourth part is you. It's not just about what's best for Marta. It's got to be about what's best for you, too." Her fingers were warm as they curled around his, and he gripped tightly, grateful for comfort he didn't really think he deserved. "What do *you* want, Alex? Can you be happy with Marta? A marriage with less passion, but more societal acceptance?"

"What's the alternative, though?" Alex didn't want to sound

pathetic, but he was pretty sure he did. "It's not… Nick isn't back here for me. He kissed me to throw me off my game, and maybe to get a bit of revenge. It wasn't about actually wanting me."

"I think you're right," Jani said firmly. "Nick's not on the table. This isn't a choice between Marta and Nick; it's a choice between Marta and the unknown. Going out and dating other men, probably. Exploring, and finding out what you like." She squeezed his hand. "It'd be terrifying, I expect. And it'd be hard to tell Marta, and hard to tell the family. But you're not afraid of doing things that are hard, not if they're what's right."

"Doing what seemed right is what lost me Nick in the first place." Alex shook his head slowly. "What the hell am I supposed to do, when I have no idea what the right thing is?"

"You're supposed to drink tea with your sister," she said. She reached for the teapot with her free hand and refilled their cups. "And probably, at some point, you should have a conversation with Marta." A quick smile. "Maybe you'll get lucky and she'll dump your cheating ass, and you won't have to make a decision after all!"

It had been meant as a joke, but the thought of Marta rejecting him shouldn't have made Alex's mind race like it did. It shouldn't have made him feel like an un-caged bird, shouldn't have felt like the removal of a heavy weight he hadn't even known he was carrying. The whole thing was too much. Alex remembered Nick's lips, hot and soft against his own, their shared breath more intimate than Alex had ever been with his fiancée, and he knew he needed to make a change. He couldn't let that one kiss be his last taste of passion for the rest of his life. Could he?

Nick's cell phone woke him up the next morning. It was 8:30, he saw, not an unreasonable time to call someone, but he was still grumpy about it. He'd gotten back to the hotel too late for a massage, and jerking off in the shower had actually made him more tense, not less. Maybe it was because of the images that had flashed through his mind as he came, the remembered sensations of almost-familiar lips opening to his. Whatever the reason, he hadn't gotten to sleep until far too late, and had tossed and turned even then.

"Nick Colton," he growled into the phone.

There was a moment's pause before a lightly accented male voice said, "It's Doctor Chutani, Mr. Colton. As we told you, we expedited your testing due to the patient's critical situation, and we have good news. The preliminary tests suggest a good chance that you'd be a match for your sister!"

"Half-sister," Nick corrected automatically. "But... *half*-sister. I looked it up, and the odds aren't supposed to be good. Are you sure on this?"

"We're sure on the preliminary test, yes. We need to perform more testing to make sure you're close enough to take the chance. Again, we wish to expedite this process. Are you available to come to the hospital for us to take more blood samples? And we'd like to perform a full physical at this time, to ensure that you're healthy enough for the procedure."

This wasn't part of the plan. Not that there'd really *been* a plan for this part of his visit. Nick had investigated the probabilities of getting a match from a half-sibling and assumed he was performing a ceremonial role. Let the parents know they'd done absolutely everything possible to save their child. He thought of the gifts he'd sent, and for the first time wondered about the actual child involved. A very sick little girl. His half-sister. Not an anonymous statistic, but a real child, vulnerable and needing help.

"It's likely because your mother and stepmother are from the same geographic region," the doctor said into the silence. "And because it was such an isolated community. They're genetically similar to each other, and you and the patient share the same father, so... you and the patient are very similar."

That was absurd. The doctor was just talking about the genetics of their bone marrow, nothing more. There was no reason for

Nick to start thinking of himself as similar to a vulnerable child, and he sure as hell didn't need anyone's help. "Okay," he said. "I'll come back down and give more blood. And get a physical, if I have to. You can't just contact my doctor in New York? I saw her a few months ago."

"For a medical condition?"

"Checkup. Everything was fine. I'm healthy."

"Excellent. We'll just double-check in case anything has changed since then."

They set up a midmorning appointment and the doctor hung up. Nick sat on the bed and stared at the phone in his hands. Bone-marrow donation. To his half-sister. The family he'd avoided so well for so long was crowding back into his life, whether he liked it or not.

This wasn't why he was in Seattle. He was supposed to be in control. He'd wanted to show everyone, including himself, that he wasn't a little boy anymore, wasn't the one scrambling to figure out things that everyone else seemed to understand by instinct. And he'd wanted to be remote; he'd wanted to be the one watching and judging as everyone else ran around in a frenzy. Instead, he was getting sucked back into it all. Bone-marrow donation. It was supposed to be safe, fairly painless… not a big deal. But he'd be under general anesthetic, which had always creeped him out. And on the few occasions when he'd been unable to avoid being put under, he'd found it made him nauseated for at least a day afterward. He'd be vulnerable, and he wasn't sure he could afford that.

He looked at the phone. It was absurd, but he knew who he wanted to call. Alex might be mad at Nick, but he wouldn't turn down a request from even a stranger in need. Surely Nick would be granted at least that much courtesy. Could Alex be with him, one person in the waiting room who cared about Nick as more than a marrow farm?

No. Nick couldn't let himself be that weak. He'd be fine. There'd probably be some logistical challenges, but he was a capable adult and he could handle them.

Or maybe there was another option. He thought a moment,

then found the number he wanted. The phone only rang once before it was picked up. "Nick? Hey, I was just thinking about you!"

"Hey, Liam. Look, I think Hawaii might be delayed a little. It's sounding like I might be a match for that bone-marrow thing after all. Any chance you're still free to come out and spend some time with me? First-class flight and some shopping, too…"

"You don't need to bribe me, babe." The words were almost convincing, but the effect was blown by Liam's total tractability. "Of course I can be there. I'll be on the next flight, even if first class is sold out. I can use your credit card?"

"Yeah." When the inevitable happened, Nick would have to remember to change that number; Liam was absolutely the sort to go on a spending spree as revenge for a breakup. "You won't be missing appointments?" Nick was regretting his invitation already. But Liam was necessary; with him in town, Alex wouldn't come anywhere near Nick, and temptation would be removed.

"No, I can get someone to cover for me." Liam was practically purring with satisfaction. "The replacement won't be quite the same, but that's okay. Better that my clients miss me than that you do."

"I'm going to have to work a lot of the time. You might be bored."

"I think you mentioned shopping, didn't you?" Liam's throaty laugh had seemed sexy the first time Nick heard it, but now it grated. "I'm sure I can keep myself entertained."

"Okay, then. I'm at the Four Seasons; I'll tell the front desk you're coming, so if I'm not around they can give you a keycard. Okay?"

"I'll see you soon, babe."

Nick disconnected the call and flopped backwards onto the bed, his hands flung out to his sides. What the hell had he just done?

CHAPTER SEVEN

Alex had wimped out and emailed Marta instead of calling her. He hadn't told her the whole story in text; he wasn't *that* much of an asshole. He'd known he should talk to her about it in person, and he hadn't been able to stand the idea of pretending to have a casual phone conversation with her while he had this big thing to discuss, so… email. He'd suggested dinner at his place, she'd agreed, and now he was in his kitchen pouring pre-chopped stir-fry ingredients into his wok as she made her way up from the lobby. He'd had a glass of wine. A big glass. And he was most of the way through another. He wondered if he should hide the bottle and open a new one to share with her so she wouldn't know how much liquid courage he'd needed, but that seemed unnecessarily dramatic. This was *Marta*. She was… Marta. She'd understand.

He'd left the door ajar so she could let herself in. He watched her kick off her shoes and wince as her heels hit the ground and her tendons stretched. Then she placed her briefcase on the floor next to her shoes, shrugged out of her suit jacket and hung it in the closet, and smiled at him as she eased onto a stool at the breakfast bar.

"Smells good," she said, reaching for the wine and pouring herself a glass.

"Just a package from the market. 'Fusion Frenzy.'" But that wasn't what he was supposed to be talking about. He drained his glass, and she looked at him curiously as she refilled it, but didn't comment.

Which left the conversation up to him. Why the hell was he cooking? Was she even going to stick around to finish the meal? Maybe he could put it off for a while. "Good day?"

"Seven hours of depositions. I can't figure out if Wilson is mentoring me or trying to turn me into a paralegal. You?"

"SeaCo takeover, all day long. Nothing really law-related;

more like being Blake's executive assistant."

"Still, lots of billable hours." She sipped her wine, made a face, and twisted the bottle to look at the label. If she didn't like it she was in luck, because Alex was just about ready to start on a second bottle. But she didn't comment on the wine. "You getting anywhere? Is it for real? Has Nick got the votes?"

It was strange to hear her speak of Nick as if she knew him, but she'd heard so many conversations among those who did, it must feel natural. And, damn it, Alex should not be thinking about what felt natural in regards to Nick! He dragged his mind back to the conversation. "It seems likely. The AGM is tomorrow night, so there's still a full day of negotiating and maneuvering, but right now, yeah. I think he has the votes."

"Damn." Marta leaned over and plucked a carrot slice from the wok, holding it between her fingernails to keep from being burned. "How's Blake taking it?"

"They think Nick's a match for Anna. Blake's... I mean, he's paying attention to the business. He's doing a good job. But his focus is definitely divided." Alex couldn't do this anymore, make small talk with the big issue hanging over his head. He turned off the heat under the wok and said, "Are you starving? Can we talk a bit before dinner?"

"It's a stir-fry, Alex. It's not going to be too tasty reheated."

"I think... this might be quick. Maybe. Or maybe we'll want a meal break to think things over." He gulped the rest of the wine in his glass and said, "I honestly have no idea how this is going to go, or what you're going to say, or how I should start..."

She frowned at him, and he could see when she realized he was talking about something important. "Okay," she said. "Grab another bottle and come sit on the couch."

He could do that. He even managed to pick out one of the bottles with a screw top so he wouldn't have to worry about finding a corkscrew. Not so long ago screw-top wine had been total rotgut, he mused. Now you could find pretty decent wine with a metal lid, and total crap with an old-fashioned cork. It was all a question of marketing, dressing things up like something they weren't. Was Alex a good wine in a screw-top bottle, or a cheap wine pretending to be classy?

"What's going on, Alex?" Marta was sitting sideways on the couch, and he knew he was supposed to sit beside her, maybe behind her so she could lean back into him, or in front so he could massage her feet. He was supposed to want to do that, want to touch her. Instead, he flopped into an armchair.

"I'm not sure." Well, that was a terrible start. He opened the wine and poured himself a healthy glass. "I just… I told you a bit about Nick Colton. About us being friends, growing up. But I never really told you that…" A big gulp of wine. "We were more than friends."

Marta's eyes narrowed a little. "More than friends. Like… brothers?"

"No." Alex had no idea where to look. Marta had a run in one of her stockings, and that was suddenly fascinating. "Like a… sexual relationship." He said the last words blurred together, much too quickly, and waited while she worked out what he meant.

"Just him?" she asked quietly.

"Yes." That was easy to say, at least, but Alex knew he wasn't finished. "But the other night. Yesterday. At the dinner. He kissed me, and I kissed him back." There was no way to put a gloss on that. No disguising what Alex had done, or what he was. Maybe he was a cheap wine in a cheap bottle; he hadn't even thought of that possibility before.

"What are you saying, Alex?" Marta wasn't calm, exactly. Well, on the surface she was, but the turmoil beneath the façade was obvious. She was a corked bottle containing a volcano instead of wine.

"I don't know. I mean, I'm saying I kissed Nick Colton last night. But I don't know what that means."

"You kissed a man. A man you've been involved with before, although you never bothered to mention that to me. And you don't know what it means?" She glared at him. "Am I supposed to *interpret* for you? Because I'll tell you what *I* think it means!"

"Please do." Alex tried to look as sincere as he felt. "I'm lost. Totally confused about the whole damned thing. If you could tell me what you think it means, that would be wonderful."

"You're serious? You're making out with men and you don't know what that means?"

"You think I'm gay." It felt strange to say the words. "That's the only way to look at this?"

It was impressive, the way she seemed to be able to keep her eyes wide in disbelief at the same time she was cynically smiling. "I don't know. How do *you* look at it?"

That was, of course, an excellent question. "I have no idea. I honestly... I didn't tell you about Nick before because you said you didn't want to do that. Remember? You said you didn't want to talk about the past, or count up scores."

"I said that because I didn't want you to think I was a slut, Alex! Not because I wanted you to hide your gay lover!"

"I would have thought you were a slut? Why? How many guys..." He stopped when he saw her expression. "Okay, probably not important right now."

"Probably not, Alex. And this isn't about before we met! This was last night! What the hell were you thinking?"

"It wasn't something I thought about! Not something I planned." Alex stopped. He couldn't fight about this, couldn't defend his behavior. "I have no idea what made me do it, Marta. I'm sorry. Sorry for last night, but for... for everything else, too."

"What's 'everything else'? What else is there?" Her voice had softened, but there was still a sharpness to her gaze that made Alex grateful he'd never been her adversary in their professional lives.

"I don't know. I think... I think I've been lying to you. To myself as well, if that makes it any better. I don't know if it does. Maybe it makes it worse."

"So." She took her own gulp of wine, and stared at it for longer than was comfortable. When she looked up, her eyes were shining. "So you're gay. That's what you're telling me. Our lackluster sex life isn't because we're both so busy and tired. It's not because you have a naturally low sex drive, or because it's *great* that my boyfriend likes to cuddle!" The self-mockery in her voice twisted in Alex's gut. He'd made her feel that way. It was his fault.

"I'm sorry, Marta. I think… yeah. I think I'm gay."

"You're thirty years old! This isn't the '50s! You couldn't have figured this out a little earlier?"

"I had it figured out when I was sixteen. No doubt in my mind." Or in his heart. Definitely none in his cock. "But I tricked myself into thinking it was something else. An infatuation with one person, instead of something fundamental in me."

"But you've been attracted to other men. If you're gay, you've seen other men over the years and found them attractive! How could you not have noticed that?"

"I think I disciplined myself not to acknowledge it." A sip of wine. Alex had been fighting with these ideas all day, but hadn't gotten too far. "I mean, I appreciated male beauty. You do that, with women. You'll say someone's really beautiful, but it doesn't mean you want to sleep with her. Lots of people do that. I just wouldn't let it go any further. I wouldn't let myself stare at a man, or fantasize about him, or anything like that."

"You're gay." Apparently Marta wasn't interested in discussing the subtleties of Alex's self-delusion. "I'm engaged to a gay man." She looked at him quickly. "Or am I? Are you breaking up with me? Are you calling it off?"

"I don't… I don't know. I assumed you'd want to. I assumed you'd have dumped a pot of stir-fry on my head and stormed out of here by now." He tried a tentative smile, but she frowned back at him. "I guess… I don't know. I mean, we should take some time to think about it, right?" He felt a rising panic. He couldn't go through this painful conversation and end up still trapped, could he? He couldn't end the engagement himself, not after hurting Marta so much already.

But to stay engaged to her… to *marry* her, now that he'd started dreaming of something else…

"I'm going home," she said firmly. "Don't call me for a couple days—I'll get back in touch when I'm ready to talk."

"Okay. Of course."

"And I know this sounds ridiculously prosaic, but I'm *starving* and the stir-fry smells good. Put some in a container for me, okay?"

Alex had always valued Marta's common sense. She had a firm grip on her emotions; she wasn't prone to extremes of joy or sorrow or anger. As he headed to the kitchen to dish up Marta's food, he wondered how Nick would have responded to something like this. Well, he already knew, he supposed. Nick would have stormed out of the city and stayed away for a damned decade. Alex shook his head. He'd never thought he'd appreciate anything about Nick's reaction, but at least one thing was clear: Nick had cared. Marta was drumming her keys impatiently on the kitchen counter as if she were in a restaurant and her take-out order hadn't been ready on time, and he could almost imagine her already thinking about the files in her briefcase, the extra work she could get done now that she didn't have to waste time socializing.

"I'm sorry, Marta," he said as he handed her the filled container.

"I'm pretty angry, Alex," she said calmly. The volcano from earlier had apparently fizzled out, or maybe been buried under more layers of stone. "And I'm hurt. But I still care about you, and I know you still care about me. I'm going to have to think about a lot of things."

"Of course. And you'll call me. If you decide anything, or you need to talk, or… anything. Right?" He couldn't believe he was saying it, but he knew Marta didn't have a lot of friends away from work, and she probably wouldn't want to share this with her colleagues. "If you don't want to talk to me, Jani's a great listener. You already know that, I guess. But I'm sure she'd be happy to help any way she can."

"You already told her?" Another one of Marta's sharp courtroom looks.

"Last night. After… you know. I was pretty confused, and I went over to talk to her about it."

"Have you told anyone else? Because if we decide to go on with the wedding, I don't think you should be advertising this. Our kids don't need to hear that about their father, down the road."

He wasn't free. She was still seriously thinking about marriage. Alex could barely string coherent words together, but he had to admit he liked the idea of keeping this quiet for a while, giving himself a chance to adjust, so he nodded. "Okay. Just Jani. She's the only person I've talked to about it, and I can keep it that way until I hear from you."

Marta winced as she stepped into her high heels. Then she reached down and picked up her briefcase before leaning over and giving Alex a quick peck on the lips just like she always did when she was leaving. It was surreal. Nothing had changed. He watched as she let herself out and walked briskly down the hallway toward the elevator.

This was really happening. He'd uncorked the bottle, and she'd screwed the lid right back on, leaving his truth trapped inside. He returned to the couch and found his wine glass, emptying it in two big gulps. He was tempted to throw it against the wall and watch it shatter into tiny fragments. Maybe that's what he'd have to do, he mused. If he couldn't escape through the expected path, maybe he'd have to smash out of his bottle. But he couldn't predict who would be hurt by flying shards. And he wasn't sure he had the strength to break out, anyway. Not when it felt so much safer inside.

CHAPTER EIGHT

They gave the son of a bitch a standing ovation. It was supposed to be Nick's victory. It *was* Nick's victory, damn it. He'd been installed as chair of the board of directors, he'd asked for and received approval for a dramatic restructuring, starting with finding a new CEO, and it had all gone smoothly. No drama, no fanfare, just business.

Then Blake had stood up. He was calm and collected, sincerely thanking the shareholders for the opportunity to work for them for so long. He expressed excitement about finding a new role for himself within the company, one with less responsibility. And he thanked them again for their support and friendship through the years. Then he sat back and smiled beatifically as the bastards surged to their feet and applauded him. Nick half expected them to rush the table and hoist the bastard onto their shoulders, carrying him around as if *he* were the one who was triumphant.

When the crowd finally settled down, the focus turned to Nick. But their faces weren't friendly anymore. Now they looked expectant. Hungry. He'd promised them something, and he needed to deliver.

He gave his own little speech, but it was essentially a reiteration of the things he'd said when he was trying to earn their votes, and he could tell they were getting restless. They wanted action immediately, wanted him to start fixing things and earning them profits right away.

Luckily, he had one plan that was already almost in place. "We need to move quickly," he said into the quiet room. "And you all know my ideas for how to improve the business's profitability. One of those ideas involves moving the production facilities. The factory is oversized for the work we're doing, and it's on prime real estate, close to downtown. It'd make more sense for us to be on the outskirts of town: less glamorous, but significantly less expensive, and more convenient for shipping."

"The factory's a landmark," Blake said dryly, and Nick figured he'd better get used to this dynamic: his father sitting back and criticizing every one of Nick's ideas. It felt familiar, but Nick was better prepared this time around.

"It doesn't have heritage designation," he replied smoothly. "There's no legal impediment to changing the land use. If community sentiment is strong enough that it would be profitable for the buyer to maintain the building's façade and restructure the interior, that would be something to be considered. By the buyer, not by SeaCo. We can't be sentimental in this economy. We need to do what makes sense for our bottom line."

"And, given the economy, you think it's a good time to be selling one of our major assets?" Blake did a good job of sounding amused and serious at the same time.

"I have a buyer in mind, and I think the board will find the offer very fair." Nick didn't bother to mention that he held a significant share in the development company he was thinking of. He'd have to deal with that later, and recuse himself from any votes on the offer, but that was a detail, not the main argument. "And we aren't selling to take profits, we're selling to reinvest. We'll buy land elsewhere, build a state-of-the-art facility, and all of those expenses will be at the same depressed prices that we might expect from our property sale."

Blake didn't respond; apparently he'd gone back to silent observation. There were a few other questions, a bit of discussion, but overall, everything went smoothly.

It had all gone exactly according to plan, Nick mused as he walked back toward the hotel. Yeah, the standing ovation had been irritating, but that was just people being kind to an old has-been. It was pity, or at best compassion. Nick didn't need that, because he wasn't weak. This was a victory. It was what he'd been working toward. But somehow, he wasn't feeling the elation he'd expected. He'd won, and he still felt empty.

His phone rang, and he immediately thought of Alex. It was

ridiculous; Alex hadn't even been at the meeting, for some reason, so he obviously didn't care much about the takeover. Which, again, was strangely disappointing, but not something Nick could dwell on. He lifted the phone and thought about not answering when he saw the number. But that was stupid.

"Hey, babe," Liam said. "The meeting over? Should I have champagne ready for the conquering hero?"

"Yeah, it went well." It *had* gone well. And there was no point in trying to explain this stupid moodiness to Liam when Nick didn't even understand it himself. "Absolutely, champagne. I'm just wrapping up a few details, but I should be back in about an hour. Sound good?"

"Sounds fantastic," Liam agreed. He had his new watch, along with several bags of clothes purchased with Nick's credit card, so he was happy.

"See you in a bit." Nick disconnected and successfully fought the urge to throw the phone against the nearest brick wall. He was being a drama queen, and there was absolutely no reason for it. So they'd given his father a standing ovation. So the old man hadn't seemed totally crushed by his defeat. So Alex hadn't even bothered to come to the meeting. So what? Nick had won. This had been a business challenge, not a personal vendetta. He'd gotten what he wanted.

Now he just needed to figure out something else to want, so he could distract himself from the hollowness of his victory. That was a good plan. He'd go back to the hotel, drink some champagne, get laid, and have a good night's sleep. The next day he'd get back to work, and he'd find something even better to strive for. Everything would be fine.

"I'm the company's lawyer," Alex said as calmly as he could. "He's the chairman of the board, and obviously intends to take an active role in the company's business. I'm going to have to work with him."

"So *work* with him." Jani had been hearing about this from Alex *and* Marta, and her patience was clearly wearing a little thin. At least this time Alex had called her at a reasonable hour. "You can work with people without making out with them, can't you?"

"In theory." Alex collapsed onto his couch but kept the phone pinned to his ear. He could imagine Jani's eyes rolling in exasperation.

"Jesus, Alex. Has Marta talked to you yet? Can you get that resolved first, and then we'll deal with this?"

"She hasn't called me. She told me not to call her. I need to give her some space, don't I? I can't start demanding answers when I'm the one who made the mess in the first place."

"What if she doesn't want to give up? What if she wants you to stay together?"

"Is that still what she's thinking? I thought she'd have gotten over that."

"I'm certainly trying to talk her out of it. It's a really stupid idea, Alex. For you *and* for her."

"I know. Except..."

"Except what?"

"All the stuff that made us a good couple before is still there, isn't it? We still have similar values, we still want similar things..."

"Yes. You both value and want *cock*. Not really the basis of a healthy heterosexual relationship, Alex."

A cruder statement than Alex would have preferred from his baby sister, but hard to argue with. "So it's over. It should be over. You're right. I just need to make her see that."

"You can make her *see* that by *telling* her that. It doesn't have to be some convoluted scheme. Just tell her."

"I feel like she should be the one to dump me. It seems like she should have that right. You know?"

"And that way it'd be a lot easier for you to not feel like the bad guy. Don't forget that part."

"That's a pretty cynical way of looking at it."

"You're considering staying in a relationship with someone with whom you are fundamentally incompatible because you're either too much of a pussy to break up with her or because you don't believe you'll ever find anything better. And you're calling *me* cynical."

"What's the right thing to do? What would a stand-up guy do in a situation like this?"

"I'm assuming you don't know how to build a time machine? Because going back and *not* getting engaged to a woman would probably be a step in the right direction."

"Are you enjoying this now? My pain is amusing to you?"

"Are you feeling pain, Alex? Yeah, you probably are. But you're feeling something else, too. Don't even try to deny it. I haven't heard you this excited, this *involved* in your own life, for a really long time. I think we both know when you lost your enthusiasm. And I don't care how much of a bastard Nick Colton is, I'm still grateful to him for waking you up." She paused, and Alex thought maybe she was appreciating the beautiful truth of her words. He certainly was. But then she cackled. "Oh my God! You were asleep for far too long, and then your prince woke you up with a kiss! You're Sleeping Beauty, Alex! You are! It's perfect!"

"It's not perfect," Alex groaned. "I'm supposed to have a princess, not a prince. I'm doing it wrong."

"Bullshit. You, brother of mine, are supposed to have a prince. Other people can have princesses, or they can wake themselves up if that's their thing. But you don't need to worry about them, just worry about you. And about your prince."

"Wait. Are you saying… are you saying *Nick Colton* is my prince? I thought he was off the table."

"Oh, he is. Probably. He's here for the wake-up call, but you can find someone else for the rest of it. I'm just saying..." He could hear her soft smile even over the phone. "I have no idea what happened to Sleeping Beauty after she woke up. I imagine she lived happily ever after, one way or another, but I don't know any of the details. But you know what she didn't do, Alex? She didn't agree to go back to sleep just because it would be simpler for everyone if she did. She stayed awake, because *that's* what she was supposed to do."

"I need to break up with Marta," Alex finally said.

"Yeah. I think you do. Because if she decides to try to work past this, and you dump her *then*? Then you're really an asshole."

"She's going to be pissed."

"She has every right to be. You fucked up, and she got hurt."

"Yeah." He sighed. "Mami and Papi are going to be pissed, too."

"*Oh* yeah," Jani agreed. "We're going to need to figure out how to spin this one, for sure. Probably tell them about the breakup and then give them a while before you spring the whole gay thing on them. Mami will figure it out, and she'll break it to Papi, and you actually saying the words will be anticlimactic after that."

It wasn't a bad plan. "Thank you, Jani. For everything. Seriously, I owe you."

"Remember when I was at my worst? And you dragged my ass to rehab and then babysat me for the first few weeks after I got out, and I swore at you and was a total fucking bitch the whole time?"

"Yeah, I remember."

"I don't owe you for that. I used to think I did, but fuck it, I don't. And you don't owe me for this. We're not trading favors here, Alex. We're family. We help each other out. Okay?"

"Yeah. Okay." There was a lump in Alex's throat that had very little to do with Janissa and even less with his impending conversation with Marta. He was thinking about Nick, growing up without this. He'd tried to find it, spending as much time as he could with Alex's family, but it hadn't been enough and he'd known it. Had Nick ever found anyone who was on his side this way, without conditions or equations? Well, he'd found Alex. And then Alex had destroyed the trust they'd shared. "I love you, Jani," Alex said.

"Damn right you do. I'm awesome." The phone disconnected and Alex stared at it a moment. He and Jani were close, but they had other siblings, too—any of whom would absolutely back him up in any way they could. He had a family, and they made him strong. Strong enough to do the difficult thing when he had to. So he took a deep breath, said a short and heartfelt prayer, and hit Marta's speed-dial. He needed to get this over with.

Of course things couldn't be that easy. Marta answered with a calm, "I asked you not to call me, Alex."

"I know. I'm sorry. But I've been talking to Jani, and I really wanted to see if we could have another conversation. You and me."

"We can. We will. But not yet."

It was pretty hard to argue with that, but also pretty hard to live with it. "I know you have a decision to make, Marta, but I have one, too, and I think you should hear about mine before you make yours."

"Fine. I won't make any decisions until I've spoken to you. But I don't want to speak to you yet."

Jesus, she was like a robot. He knew it was her defense mechanism, and he respected it, mostly. She was being respectful and sane, and if she ever decided she needed a break from the law she could probably write a very empowering advice column about maintaining personal boundaries. Alex just wanted the whole thing to be settled and done.

But he wasn't the victim here. This wasn't supposed to be about what *he* wanted. "Okay," he said finally. "I'm sorry."

"Okay," she replied.

"Do you have any idea when…" he began, but stopped speaking when he heard the sound of the line being disconnected. She'd hung up on him. She had every right to, but that didn't make it any easier for him to unclench his fingers from his own phone and set it calmly down on the table. He wasn't free. He hadn't escaped. And he had no idea how much longer he could stand it.

CHAPTER NINE

"I want to talk to you."

Nick whirled to see his father's wife flying down the hospital corridor like an eagle with prey in sight. Damn, the woman was imposing when she wanted to be. He refused to step back, instead smiling stiffly and saying, "Helena. Or do you prefer Mrs. Colton? Either way, I assume you've heard the good news?"

Nick was still coming to grips with the information himself. He was a match. Not perfect, but close enough that the doctors wanted to go ahead with the procedure. And they wanted to do it as soon as possible, while the girl still had a little strength left.

"I heard," Helena said.

"I know we don't know each other, but… you don't seem pleased. Is there a problem?"

She stared at him fiercely. "You're the problem. You and your games; your stupid, childish need to hurt your father. But this is my *daughter* we're talking about here, and you will *not* play games with her." She hadn't touched him, but her hands were balled into tight, sharp-looking fists and she was standing about six inches away, staring up at him like she might attack at any second.

Nick tried to keep his voice calm. "I honestly have no idea what you're talking about."

"You don't? Do you know that if you agree to the transplant, they put her on a round of *intense* chemotherapy, right away? Probably some radiation, too. To kill every last bit of her own bone marrow. Right now, she's still got a few cells in there doing their jobs, but for the transplant to work they have to make sure it's a completely sterile field before they plant the seeds from you."

Nick didn't really like the image of his seeds being planted in a prepubescent girl, but he tried to pull his mind out of the gutter. "Yeah, I read about that. I did quite a bit of research on this, you know. And they've been showing me videos like they think I'm on the jury at Cannes. I think I understand the procedure."

"Do you?" She stepped a little closer and, pride be damned, Nick backed up. "Do you understand that without viable bone marrow, she'll die? If they kill what little she's got, and her body can't produce anything new, and you don't *supply* something new, she'll die." There was a jagged edge on the last word that showed the frantic mother behind the intense warrior, and it was enough to help Nick stay calm.

"I know. I understand."

"And what are you planning to do about it? Wait until they start the chemo, and then make some outrageous demand in exchange for your donation?"

"Jesus Christ, lady! You seriously think…" Nick caught himself. *Worried mother. Worried mother.* He repeated it like a mantra and took a deep breath. "You haven't got anything I want. Neither does Blake. Even if he did, I wouldn't hold a child hostage to get it. I've agreed to the transplant, I've made an appointment for the procedure, and that's it. I'm done. No games, no demands."

"Because you love your family so much?" She still sounded bitter, but there was a trace of hopefulness in her voice. She *wanted* to believe.

"Fuck family." He let his eyes go cold, but she didn't look away. "I can help save a little girl's life. That's it, that's all. Related or not, it doesn't matter to me." They stared at each other for a moment, and then he threw his hands up in the air. "Believe me or don't. Your call. But I have an appointment for Tuesday morning, and I'll be there. That's all I can say."

"I want you to meet her." Her eyes stayed locked on his. "I want you to look her in the face, and recognize your little sister, and know that it's her life at stake."

"Half-sister. And I really don't see the point. If you think I'm enough of an asshole to walk away after going this far, why would you think spending five minutes with a kid who's probably too sick to do more than lie there is going to change me?"

"It'll be the start of the curse I'll be building to put on you if you betray her faith. If you don't do what you should, I will curse you to see her innocent face every day for the rest of your life. I'll curse you to have that face ruin all your moments of joy and deepen all your moments of sorrow. I'll—"

"Stop." The curse bullshit wasn't intimidating, but Nick was overwhelmed anyway. "You… you really are from the same place as her. As my mother. She used to talk like that, too."

"Yes." Helena sounded annoyed by the interruption. "We grew up in the same village. We're cousins."

"So she's not only my half-sister, she's also my second cousin." Nick didn't actually *say* that it was pretty gross, but he was sure the message got across.

"I met your father when he came to return your mother's ashes to the family plot. Years after her death. Apparently his beloved son had just abandoned him and he was trying to find some closure and peace."

"His beloved son? Damn, I knew he had two families, but I didn't know he'd found time for a third. Anyway, you met him, and you helped him find peace. And he helped get you out of some poor-ass backwater Greek village. Sounds like a good deal for everyone."

"Do you hear me speaking, asshole? Do I sound like an ignorant peasant? I learned English at a British boarding school, and I was home on vacation from doing my Masters at UCLA when I met your father. I didn't need his *help* to escape from one of the most beautiful places on earth. I fell in love with him!"

"Well, that's a really romantic story. Truly. I'm touched. And I'm sorry for interrupting the curse preview. Did you want to get back to that, or can I carry on with my day? I have quite a few appointments—it takes a *lot* of time to dig a company out from under years of mismanagement."

"You're an arrogant son of a bitch."

It was as if she was daring him. She *wanted* him to get angry and threaten to withdraw from the donation procedure, so her low opinion could be confirmed. He smiled at her. "I'm the arrogant son of a bitch who's going to save your daughter's life. Not to mention her inheritance."

"I want you to meet her." For the first time, there was a note of pleading in the woman's voice. "I need to know… I need to believe that you won't let her down. Whatever is between you and Blake, I need to know you don't hate him so much that you'd make an innocent little girl suffer."

Nick stared at her. "I don't hate him at all. That's not what… that's not what this was about." There were tears in her eyes, now— not out yet, thank God, but threatening. Nick couldn't deal with that. He needed to get out of there, but her hand was on his arm, gentle but strong.

"Five minutes. That's all. She wants to meet you. Her brother." She stopped, then said, "Half-brother," as if the extra syllable was a gift. "She has no energy, so she won't keep you long. But she liked the presents. And she's curious about you. Please."

This was absolutely not in the plan. But, damn it, what had the plan done for him lately? "Five minutes," he said cautiously. "Unless she's asleep or something. I don't want to disturb her, and I can't wait around all day."

"Okay," Helena agreed readily, and that was how Nick found himself being guided down to the pediatric oncology ward, dressed in a mask and gown, and escorted into a private room. The girl in the bed was too small. Not short, and too covered up to tell if she was skinny, but small. Shrunken, like there wasn't enough life in her for her body to fully inflate. Nick liked the idea of taking a little of his energy and finding a better home for it.

"Anna, sweetie," Helena said softly, and the girl's eyes flew open. She stared at Nick, and Helena said, "This is Nick. He wanted to come say hello. Is that okay?"

The girl smiled at him, and Nick wondered how he'd ever thought she was lacking energy. Her face shone with the light of a thousand suns now, and she said, "Nick!" Then she looked at her mother and suddenly turned bashful. "It's nice to meet you," she said, but she wouldn't look back in his direction.

"Nice to meet you, too. Sorry you're stuck in here, but maybe we can do something when you get out." Where the hell had that come from? He had no intention of ever seeing this kid again. Did he?

"How did you know I like horses?" she asked.

He was temporarily confused, then remembered the gifts he'd sent up. They'd been books, mostly; some stickers, and a stuffed animal. Maybe a horse... who the hell knew? "Lucky guess?" he suggested, and then just to tweak her mother a little he added, "Or maybe a mystical sibling bond. Maybe I can just tell some things about you, because we're related." Maybe the girl in the gift shop knew horses were a safe bet for an eight-year-old girl.

But Adrianna was nodding seriously. "I think that's it," she said. "I know things about Damon, sometimes."

She could sometimes guess things about the kid she'd lived with for six years? Wow, she must be psychic. But Nick kept his smile on and said, "That's nice. To have someone that close to you."

"It'll be bad for him, though." She glanced almost furtively at her mother, then turned back to Nick. "If I don't get to go home. He'll be lonesome." She stared at Nick as if waiting for something, but what the hell was he supposed to say to an eight-year-old facing her own mortality? "Maybe you could help with that?" she suggested, as if the answer should have been obvious to him. "Maybe he'd feel better if he had a new brother?"

Nick could not do this. He snuck a peek at Helena, whose smile was fixed on her face as if she'd heard and endured similar conversations in the past. "I don't think we need to worry about that," he said quickly. He had no idea what the proper psychological approach was. Maybe he was leading the kid down an unhealthy path, but what the hell? Denial had always worked well enough for him. He eased a little closer and gave her his best smile before remembering that most of his face was covered by a surgical mask. He dropped his voce as if telling her a secret. "My bone marrow is, like, super-charged. No joke—I'm hardly ever sick. This is some primo stuff you're going to be getting out of me. Give it enough time to work, and Damon is going to be wishing he could settle you down a little, you're going to be so out of control with energy. He won't be missing you, he'll be missing his peace and quiet."

"Super-charged," she said softly. Even this short visit had clearly tired her, and it was surprisingly difficult to watch her energy draining away.

"No joke," Nick said with conviction.

"No joke," she echoed. She looked at her mother. "Is that true, Mommy? It's going to be super-charged?"

"No joke," Helena said. The curve of her smile was clear even through the mask, and her eyes were only a little shinier than usual. "We'll have to get you that pony, so you have somewhere to go and burn off a bit of your energy."

"Might need to race the horse," Nick suggested. "Not like a race horse, but, like, you on the ground, the horse on the ground, and see who goes faster." And again, just because he could, he said, "And hopefully you'll have a dog, if you don't have one already. I always wanted a dog when I was a kid, but Blake didn't like animals in the house." He smiled sweetly at Helena. "But I think a dog would be *great* for a kid with super-charged bone marrow."

"No joke," Anna said to her mother. "A puppy."

"Puppies grow into big dogs," Helena replied, frowning at Nick. "But maybe Nick would like to have a dog at his house. If he thinks it's such a great idea."

"I don't have a house," Nick told Anna. "Just an apartment. No room for a dog."

"No room for kids, either?" The little girl wasn't quite fishing for an invitation, but she seemed interested in the idea.

And that was a bit complicated. "There's a spare bedroom. I guess kids could stay in there. But it's really far away. All the way on the other side of the country, touching the other ocean."

"That's far," Anna said seriously. "Don't you get lonely?"

It was stupid. Ridiculous. But Nick couldn't look at her pale, sad face and tell her anything but the truth. And once he said it to her, he had to hear it himself. "Yeah. Sometimes I do get lonely."

Anna's smile was kind and accepting. "You don't have to anymore. Me and Damon can visit you, and keep you company."

"With the dog," Helena said sweetly.

"And maybe my pony!" Anna added. She giggled, and her mother laughed.

Nick needed to get the hell out of there. "I have somewhere I need to be, Anna, but it was really nice meeting you. I'll be sure to eat lots of really healthy food for the next couple days, okay? Then when they take the marrow out, it'll be even more super than usual."

"Spinach?" she asked with a wrinkled nose.

"You bet. I'll eat it so you don't have to. Deal?"

"No joke."

Helena guided him out, and when Nick looked back through the big window, Anna's eyes were already closed. "A dog *and* no spinach?" Helena asked with a smile.

"You better keep me away from her; the next time I see her, I'm promising driving lessons. And a unicorn."

"You won't let her down." It was phrased as a statement, but the doubt was still clear in Helena's voice.

This was getting stupid, and Nick decided it was time to address the issue head on. "What do you actually know about me? First-hand, I mean, not filtered through whatever crap my father is telling you?"

"Blake? Blake barely says your name, and when he does, it's all about how he let you down, and how he messed up." She stared at him. "Lately, he's been mentioning your business acumen, and wondering where you picked it all up. I don't have a negative opinion of you because of anything Blake's said." Her eyes grew fierce again, and Nick could tell that their truce was over. "It's because of all the things he *doesn't* say. He never says, 'Nick called and wished me a happy birthday.' Or 'I think I'll see if Nick wants to go golfing with me.'" She frowned at him. "I don't hear any of that. So, no, don't blame your father for me thinking you're impulsive and selfish. I came to that conclusion all on my own."

"Okay, then." Nick wasn't going to stand in the hallway outside some kid's hospital room and fight with this woman about whether he was or wasn't a worthless human being. "I gave you your five minutes. I have been touched and moved by your brave child. Are you satisfied? Is it okay for me to leave now, or do I need to do some more penance before you allow me the privilege of undergoing the surgery?"

She was silent for a moment, and when she spoke, the heat was gone from her voice. "You won't let her down?" she asked.

"I won't. I'll be there." It was all he could offer. If it wasn't enough, she'd have to find someone else to give her what she needed.

But she seemed satisfied, at least temporarily. "She needs you. We all do."

And Nick was back to feeling like a bone-marrow factory. "Okay. I understand."

He understood all too well, he mused as he found his way out of the hospital. This game they'd been playing, pretending that Nick had been unreachable... it was silly. His Christmas cards had carried postmarks from the start; he hadn't made any real effort to hide. If they'd wanted to find him, they could have. That was clear; as soon as they'd needed him, they'd been able to track him down with no trouble.

He'd left. He'd take responsibility for that, inasmuch as it carried any weight of guilt. But he'd stayed away because no one had asked him to come back. And when they did ask, it was because of a freak of genetics, not because they wanted *him*. He was an adult. He wasn't going to feel sorry for himself, and he wasn't going to dig up old hurts. Much. But that didn't mean it was all better. It didn't mean they'd suddenly be a happy family, when they had never been that before.

And it sure as hell didn't mean he was going to ride along on the guilt trip precious Miss Helena was conducting. He'd help the little girl if he could. That was it. He wasn't going to let Helena manipulate him into spending time with the kids. It was strange, though. The way she'd been talking, it almost felt like she'd been offering the family up not as a punishment, but as a reward.

Whatever. He had more important things to think about. Real things, as in real estate. He headed off toward the hotel, looking forward to getting some work done. And maybe a quickie, if Liam was around. That was the right way forward. He didn't need to get bogged down with sick eight-year-olds, not when he could be having sex and making sweet business deals. Everything was good. Everything was completely fine.

He tried not to think about how often he was having to reassure himself of those facts, these days.

CHAPTER TEN

"It's all about the real estate." Alex wasn't sure whether he was bringing good news or bad, but he was so relieved to have figured it out that he barely cared how Blake took the news. "He owns a significant share in the corporation that's offering to buy the factory property. He's trying to make a profit from both sides."

Blake stared at him. Apparently this was *not* good news. "He wouldn't be so stupid. Would he?" Blake stood up and paced around his oak-paneled home office. He still had space at the SeaCo building, but he was spending less and less time there.

It was easier for Alex to figure out who to bill when he could base the decision on the geography of the meeting. He worked for Blake Colton, and he worked for SeaCo. So far, he hadn't seen any conflict of interest. If he'd worked for *Nick* Colton, though… "It would seem he *is* that stupid. He hasn't done anything actionable yet, as far as I can tell. But he's heading toward a clear conflict of interest, breach of fiduciary duty—any number of grounds for lawsuits. Not to mention possible issues with the SEC or other federal regulators." Alex should have felt a lot more satisfied than he did. He'd done his job. He'd found a problem. But one look at Blake's face made it clear the discovery was not welcome.

"Why would he take that chance?" Blake mused.

Alex frowned. This was getting complicated. He'd been proud of himself, pushing away personal feelings and focusing on the research and legalities. But now it came back to him like a wave. This was Nick. It wasn't some anonymous upstart, poking his nose in and waiting to be crushed by the weight of authority. It was Nick. Who had never had much respect for authority in the first place…

"I need to talk to him," Blake said firmly, but as soon as he'd spoken, his face showed doubt. "Or would that just make him more stubborn? Make him more reckless? Damn it, what the hell is he thinking?"

"Maybe he has a plan. As far as we know, what he's done is questionable, but not illegal. He may have something in mind. We might be overreacting."

Blake just gave him a look. "It's *Nick*. Doing something foolish. You really think he has a long-term plan?"

"He managed to take your company away from you, and seemed to plan that out pretty meticulously." Alex knew he'd crossed a line as soon as the last syllable faded from his lips, but he didn't regret it. Blake was thinking of Nick as one thing, and they had good reason to believe he'd changed into something else altogether. It would have been irresponsible of Alex not to point that out.

"How's your personal life, Alex?"

It was a strange question, and Alex stared at Blake in surprise before managing, "Why do you ask?"

Blake snorted. "Because the last time I saw you and Nick together, you looked like he'd shoved a snake up your ass."

Well, that was some evocative language. Alex couldn't decide whether it was quaintly folksy or nastily homophobic. Either way, it wasn't an image he wanted to dwell on. "Everything's fine, thanks."

"You and Marta are good?" Blake's gaze was too pointed to be casual, so there was no point in dreaming up a lie.

"Not really, no. But that's about me, not Nick. And I don't think it's relevant to the business at hand. Nick is about to embroil the company in a mess of securities violations, lawsuits, and other complications. What are we going to do about that?"

"We're going to stop him," Blake said easily. He'd been frowning while Alex equivocated about his personal life, but his forehead was unwrinkled now.

"We're going to warn him off?"

"Oh, no," Blake replied, leaning back until his leather chair creaked in protest. "Nothing that straightforward. I mean, can you imagine Nick taking a warning from me as anything other than a dare? He wouldn't listen, that's for sure." He shook his head almost sadly, but his smile was sharp. "When I say we're going to stop him, I mean we're going to *beat* him."

Alex wasn't sure he wanted to hear any more, but he doubted he had a choice. Blake was a loving father, but his pride had been wounded. Alex knew the Colton men too well to believe either of them would walk away from a fight.

Nick was trying to keep his mind on business, but it wasn't easy. He was starving, banned from eating prior to the surgery, and he was anticipating the terrifying lack of control that would come from being in the hospital, and especially from the anesthesia. And at a deeper level, he wondered if his bone marrow would be enough. That little girl, helpless and brave, lying there waiting for him to rescue her. The doctors had said he wasn't a perfect match. Good, they'd said. Worth trying, but only because they were so desperate, because nothing else had worked and the kid would die without this treatment. She'd die. A little girl who loved ponies and her brother and her mother—and probably her father, although Nick had no independent evidence of that—would die if his bone marrow didn't work in place of hers. He looked down at his hips and willed the marrow to be compliant. *Just get along, you stubborn bastards,* he told the cells. *She's a good kid. She'll take care of you. Vegetables and exercise. Don't fuck with her.*

"Nick?" He looked up to see Andrea Dean peering at him with a mix of curiosity and exasperation. "You with us? This is pretty important stuff."

"I'm with you." Andrea had been his lawyer for years, and she knew him well enough to know when he was off his game. But he hoped she also knew he'd pull it together when he had to.

"You need to do this deal clean," she said firmly. "That means you will abstain from any SeaCo voting on the matter, and you will be absolutely upfront about your involvement in both companies. There's nothing *de facto* illegal about you having shares in two companies that are doing business with each other, but people are going to be giving the deal some serious scrutiny. You need to be above reproach or we could be tied up with legal wrangling for far too long."

"I've got it. I'm good." He saw her scrutiny and frowned. "It's not a guaranteed deal. I can recommend it in good faith, but things are volatile over there. Blake is still an unknown, and the board members are edgy. They want to make money, so they should be okay, but…" It hurt to admit, but he couldn't ignore it. "Blake's a big factor. They feel guilty for kicking him out, and they might do something stupid to show they still love him."

"But you're making them love *you*," Andrea said with a smile. "The medical thing is a good move. One more way you're rescuing the old man. And it's totally removed from the company, so there's no worry about conflicts of interest or anything else improper. You should make the most of it. Make sure everyone knows about it."

Nick was pretty damn sure he wasn't going to do that. Maybe after the fact, when he was feeling stronger. But no way was he going to advertise his vulnerability—not to the Seattle crowd, and not to anyone else.

Including Andrea. "I've got it under control," he said firmly. "But I need to get going. Thanks for meeting me so early, but I've got to run." He wouldn't let himself think about what he was running *to*, not yet. "I think I'll need to take tomorrow off, but I'll call you, and I'll see you for sure the day after," he said to Andrea. "Keep an eye on things for me, but keep it clean. You're right; I don't want lawsuits and securities bullshit. Okay?"

"You got it, boss," she said with a little flip of her fingers as a salute. Nick trusted her. He had to.

Damn it, he thought, nothing to prevent him from going to the hospital. No last-minute crisis, no challenge from a disgruntled shareholder. Just him and his appointment with a needle. He thought about calling Liam and asking him to come along; the hospital had said Nick should be ready to return home that night, as long as he had someone to look after him. And Liam was delighted to be that someone. But Liam wouldn't be any comfort now. He'd be a pain in the ass, most likely. So Nick straightened his shoulders and headed to his fate alone, as he always had.

Nick looked like he was walking toward the executioner's block, but he kept moving forward. Alex fell in beside him. He knew it was stupid, and he'd been cursing himself all the way to the hospital, but he'd still come. Nick was having surgery, and Alex couldn't just ignore that and go on with his day. It was strange, but it seemed right to be there.

"You feeling okay?" he asked.

"I had a physical on Thursday. No fresh symptoms since then." Nick was staring straight ahead, storming through the hospital lobby like he was a GI on D-Day.

"I didn't mean medically." Alex tried to think of the magic words that would make this all make sense, but he couldn't find them. "I meant *you*."

Nick ground to a halt, but it was only because they had reached the elevator bank. "Are you getting metaphysical on me, Alex? The mind/body divide? Is that what you're getting at?"

"What? No. I don't think so. I just meant... you know..."

"Law school, Alex. Where they teach you how to use words effectively. You *graduated*, didn't you?"

The elevator arrived, and Alex stepped inside after Nick. They rode in silence for a couple floors, and then Alex said, "Are you nervous?"

Nick's eyes were impossibly blue and infinitely deep. He looked at Alex, and for just a moment, a beautiful, cursed moment, it was like the last decade hadn't happened and it was still Nick and Alex against the world. But Nick blinked and shutters fell, and when he said, "It's a routine procedure," Alex knew he was getting a pat response.

"Still scary, though," he tried, but Nick just lifted his

eyebrows.

"I think Helena's planning to be there, if you need someone's hand to hold."

"Come on, Nick…"

"No." Nick's voice wasn't loud, but it was intense enough to make the other man in the elevator turn to stare and then quickly turn away. Nick snarled at the back of the man's head, then told Alex, "You don't get to do that. You can't play both sides."

"What do you—"

"You're fired," Nick said quickly. "As counsel for SeaCo Toys. I don't think it was a good idea for you to have been working for my father and the company at the same time, and it sure isn't a good idea for you to keep doing it now that he's no longer CEO."

Alex tried not to react. SeaCo was his only big account, his only evidence that he could be a rainmaker and bring clients to the firm. But he had to look past that, at least temporarily. He was at the hospital for something more important. "Okay," he said. "Have the new lawyer contact me and I can see about transferring the files." He paused as the elevator stopped moving and they both watched the other rider step onto his floor with only a quick backward glance.

"That's it?" Nick asked as the doors slid closed. "No drama, no last-minute sales pitches?"

"No. It's fine. That's not why I'm here." And then there were no more words, no more thoughts, because Nick had rolled his body toward Alex's, and his strong hand reached out to find Alex's unresisting head, and then their lips were joined, again, as they always should have been, Nick's tongue strong and sensuous as Alex opened to him, their joint gasps each swallowed by the other.

It was only a couple of floors before the elevator dinged again, and Nick pulled away before the tone faded. "For luck," he said quickly as he stepped out of the elevator. It made Alex remember a young Nick, lower leg broken beyond recognition after a stupid stunt with a skateboard and a two-story drop. It had been before they'd gotten physical, but Nick had clung to Alex's hand with desperate strength as the doctors examined him and prepped him for surgery. Alex had only been allowed to stay because Nick had refused to let go of him. It hadn't been the pain, Alex had recognized even then. Nick was afraid of the oblivion of anesthesia, terrified of fading into the same drug-induced haze that had taken his mother's life. Of course, her descent into nothingness had been deliberate, but she'd worked up to the big event with smaller ventures, and Nick had seen her in the midst of too many of them.

"You'll be okay," he said now, just as he had said in the past. "They're pros. I'll see you when you come out, and you'll be fine. Okay?"

For a moment Alex wasn't sure Nick was hearing him, but then the familiar cocky grin reappeared. "I'm good," Nick said. "Everything's good."

"I'll be in the waiting room," Alex said.

"You don't have to," Nick started, but then he stopped, and said, "Yeah. Thank you. If you have time."

"I just got fired from my biggest account," Alex said with a grin that would have created apoplexy in his supervising partners. "I've got lots of time."

Nick looked temporarily startled, then returned the smile. "Silver lining," he said with a wise nod.

"Looking on the bright side," Alex agreed. His mouth—hell, his whole body—was still burning and tingling from Nick's kiss, but that wasn't the current topic. "And you'll be fine. They'll take good care of you."

"When they say 'pelvic bones' and 'lower back,' do you think they mean 'ass'?" Nick was moving, but it was slow, and his eyes were still locked on Alex's. "'Cause they're going at it from behind, apparently, and I really can't figure a way to get to my pelvis from behind that doesn't involve some ass contact."

"Upper ass, maybe," Alex tried. "With the needles on a slant."

Nick's hands flew up to cover his ears. "I'm not thinking about the n-word," he explained earnestly.

"Since when are you worried about ass contact, anyhow?" This felt dangerous, but too exciting and tempting to ignore. Alex had never really flirted with anyone, but he was pretty sure that's what he was doing now. "I seem to recall you being pretty relaxed about flashing it around."

"I need to keep it perfect," Nick said, his face still serious. "Don't want it scarred up or anything."

"Maybe you should emphasize that to the doctors before you go in. They might be too professional to notice that they're working on an ass with such artistic merit, and not give it proper respect."

"You're probably right," Nick said. "Damn, do you think my ass needs a lawyer, to look out for its interests? I hear some time just opened up in your schedule." His expression was strange when he added, "But I guess that would still be a conflict of interest, you representing both my ass and the man who wants to kick it."

They were standing at some sort of nurse's station, waiting for the woman in front of them to finish her business; it wasn't really the place for a deep conversation. But this seemed important, so Alex shifted around until he was standing in front of Nick and had his full attention. "You're trying to save his daughter's life," he said seriously. "He has no interest in kicking your ass. Kissing it, maybe. Not kicking."

Nick smiled sadly. "Okay, José," he said in a voice that made it clear that he didn't believe a word Alex was saying.

"Don't call me José."

"Why not? I always used to."

"And I always hated it. It's borderline racist."

"No. Is it? I don't think so. It's... is it?"

"Maybe not." Alex had no idea why he'd brought this up, and he was pretty sure he never wanted to talk about it again.

But Nick didn't seem interested in dropping the subject. "I'm sorry," he said, and he sounded genuine. "If you thought it was racist, or even if you just didn't like it. Sorry."

"It's not a big deal, Nick."

"No, I want… you know, before the surgery…"

"Jesus Christ, Nick, you're not going to die!" That came out a little louder than it should have, and Alex looked around guiltily before saying in a quieter voice, "It's a routine procedure in a reputable hospital. You're young and healthy. It's probably more dangerous for you to have driven to the hospital than it is for you to have the surgery."

"I didn't drive. I walked."

"I have no idea how that affects the statistics. But the important thing is, you're going to be fine."

Nick stared at him for longer than was polite, but Alex didn't look away. Finally, Nick said, "I fucking hate general anesthesia."

"Yeah." There wasn't much else for Alex to say.

Nick nodded slowly, then turned toward the waiting nurse. "I have to check in. I did most of it downstairs, but they said I had to come up here for the rest. I'm Nick Colton." He glanced back at Alex briefly, grinned quickly and only a little queasily, then turned back to the nurse and said, "I'm really looking forward to the procedure."

CHAPTER ELEVEN

Nick woke up slowly. One of the reasons he hated general anesthesia so much was that it clearly hated him back. He had no food in his stomach to throw up, but that didn't keep his body from trying a few times. He was disoriented, confused, dizzy and miserable. The overhead lights were too bright, the sounds of the hospital were strange and frightening, and he was all alone.

"Steady, Nick." Warm pressure on his shoulder, and Nick looked over to see a familiar face, but not the one he'd half expected. "You're okay," Blake said calmly.

"Wha?" The word wasn't exactly clear in Nick's head, but it was definitely more coherent than the sound he managed to produce.

"Only family in the recovery room," Blake explained. "So Alex gave me a call."

"Wahm…" On that one, Nick wasn't even sure what he'd been trying to say.

"You're okay. The procedure was successful. They're processing the donation now, and they'll do the transfusion in a couple of hours."

A long wait as Nick gathered his energy and focus, and then, "Dzzzt?"

Blake raised an eyebrow. "I don't know what you're saying, Nick. It probably isn't important. Go back to sleep, and when you wake up you'll be more coherent."

But maybe it *was* important. Maybe this wasn't the natural aftereffects of the anesthetic; maybe this was the beginning of an adverse reaction, Nick's body shutting down. Or maybe there'd been some sort of brain damage and this was as clear as Nick was ever going to get. "Whungz," he insisted. "Dabbbst…"

"Go to sleep," his father replied. Nick didn't think that was a good idea at all, but his body apparently disagreed, and he drifted off.

His next awareness was of being held down, strange hands on his chest and his legs, a loud, unfamiliar voice saying, "Calm down, Mr. Colton. You're fine. Relax, Mr. Colton. Please."

But where was he, and who the hell was talking to him, and how was he supposed to relax when they were pushing him, driving him back into the darkness, keeping him where he didn't want to be?

"Chill out, Nick." Nick's eyes opened and scanned the room desperately. There was the familiar face, a worried frown above an open mouth, and Nick heard it again. "You're okay. It's okay. They're trying to help."

"Alex," Nick managed, and as his body relaxed the hands eased away from him, leaving room for Alex to edge a little closer.

"Your dad had to go. Anna's having the transfusion. They thought you'd be asleep for longer."

"Alex," Nick said again.

"You are so fucked up, Nick." Alex turned to the nearest nurse and said, "He's not good with anesthesia, but this seems extra messy. Is he okay?"

"His vital signs are good. He's just having a hard time in his head. Sometimes it happens. As long as he stops flailing around, he should be fine. It'll go away shortly."

"You hear that, Nick?" Alex leaned over Nick's head and peered at him in concern. "Just sit tight, and you'll be okay."

"Just family," Nick mumbled. He wasn't too sure what he was talking about, but Alex nodded his head.

"Apparently, when a patient goes totally ape-shit, they make an exception. Good to know, really."

"Stay," Nick said. He was pretty sure he'd meant it to be a question, or even a disavowal of the 'You don't have to' variety. But just the one word came out, and Alex nodded in response.

"Yeah. Okay. Until you're back to yourself. I'll stay." He reached behind him and pulled up a chair. After he sat down, he reached out and gently gripped Nick's forearm.

Nick let himself drift away. He still felt as if a giant had picked him up and shaken him vigorously, then spun him around about fifty times and kicked him in the head for good measure, but he just felt rotten, not afraid. Alex was there. And Alex would stay.

Nick had been a hell of a lot more pleasant when he was drugged, Alex decided. Not that he was aggressive now, just sullen. There was none of the little-boy-lost element that had made his post-anesthesia behavior appealing rather than annoying, and without that...

"I'm fine," Nick grumbled. It was all he'd been saying since they'd left the hospital. "Liam's at the hotel. I could have gotten him to pick me up. I'm fine."

"You called, and he didn't answer." Alex didn't want to think too much about this Liam, but he had a low opinion of anyone who wouldn't be sitting by the phone waiting for news. Or, even better, pacing around the damned waiting room. "There's no way I'm going to leave you sitting in the hospital, waiting for some flake who can't even pick up a damn call." Oops. That had been a bit more than he'd meant to say.

But Nick didn't seem worried about it. "Yeah," he sighed. "You had other stuff to do today, though."

"Nothing that can't wait. This is more important."

"The little girl's okay?"

"Anna." Alex had no idea why Nick refused to use her name. "She's fine, so far. Her part of this isn't as dramatic as yours. She just got a blood transfusion, essentially. They'll be giving her drugs to make sure she doesn't reject your cells, and other than that, we all just have to wait and hope the transplant takes hold."

"Super-charged," Nick said randomly. The anesthetic wasn't

entirely out of his system, apparently.

The cab pulled up in front of the hotel, and Alex paid the driver over Nick's vague and unfocused objections. He watched as Nick dragged himself out of the back seat and trudged into the hotel, then trailed after him. He felt unnecessary and unwanted, but he'd committed to seeing Nick safely home. Or wherever he was calling home.

The hotel was certainly stylish enough, all clean modern lines and wide expanses of glass, but it was hard to imagine it as a place to rest and recover. Alex thought of his own apartment and wondered if it was really any better. Not that there was any reason to think about taking Nick there. Not that Nick was his to take anywhere.

They rode the elevator in silence, and Alex refused to think of a similar trip at the hospital earlier in the day. Nick had been wound up, then, nervous and looking for a distraction. That was all. Currently, Nick was about as sexy and impulsive as a wet kitten.

They made it down the hall without incident, but Nick slumped against the wall outside the door to his room and closed his eyes rather than digging out his keycard. Alex let him gather his energy for a while, then gently asked, "Do you need help?"

"I feel like crap. And my back hurts."

"That sucks. It'll be better if you're lying down, hopefully. Is your keycard in your wallet?"

"My mouth tastes like rotten shit."

"That's very vivid. And repulsive. Where's the keycard?"

"My skull feels like it's too big in the front," he mumbled pathetically, "and too small in the back."

"Nick!" Alex didn't want to yell at a sick friend, but this was getting stupid. "The keycard."

Nick finally heaved himself off the wall and fumbled groggily until he found his wallet. He flipped it open and then apparently ran out of interest, thrusting the whole thing impatiently in Alex's direction.

Thankfully, the keycard was clearly visible, because Alex really didn't want to burrow through Nick's wallet. Well, a part of him wanted to. A part of him wanted to empty the damn thing on the bedspread and sort through every scrap inside looking for any possible clues about Nick's life for the last decade. But the better part of him, the part he tried to listen to most often, was relieved to pull the card out and flip the wallet shut.

A quick swipe, a beep, and Alex pushed the door open before prodding Nick forward. Should he offer his shoulder for support? But Nick was moving, slowly making his way through the doorway and into the room. Alex trailed after him, but stopped when he saw the lean, shirtless man—Liam, presumably—rise gracefully from an armchair by the window.

"Babe!" the stranger exclaimed. "You're back! You were supposed to call me."

Nick ignored him. He stumbled toward the bed and collapsed onto it, face buried in the bedspread, and didn't move.

"He *did* call," Alex said. "There was no answer."

The man frowned, then said, "I must have been in the shower. Or at the gym." He gave a quick look at Nick, then crossed the room with his hand extended. "I'm Liam, Nick's boyfriend. You are…?"

"Alex." He ignored the "boyfriend" designation and the man's shirtless comfort. That was none of his business. "Nick doesn't do well with anesthetics. The hospital cleared him to come home, but they said he needs to be watched closely." Alex didn't have a good feeling about this. "Can you do that? Like, no more trips to the gym or whatever. Can you just sit here and read or something until we're sure he's okay? And there's an aftercare list; he can take care of it on his own tomorrow, probably, but for tonight…"

"Of course I can do it. When Nick knew he was going to need to be taken care of, he called me to help out." Liam was clearly pleased about that. He turned away from Alex and leaned down beside Nick's bed, smoothing Nick's hair back from his face with a familiarity Alex didn't want to envy. "You're okay now, babe. I'll take care of you."

Nick responded with an indistinct grunt, and Liam turned his head toward Alex. "I'm sorry, but who are you, again? Alex who? Do you work for the hospital? Or for Nick?"

"I'm an old friend. Nick and I grew up together." Alex waited curiously for the reaction.

"Oh." Liam didn't seem too impressed. "I never got the impression that Nick was in touch with anyone from his childhood. I thought he was happy to cut those ties when he got the hell out of Seattle."

Well, that was straightforward. And a good reminder for Alex. He'd invited himself into Nick's life at a vulnerable moment, but there was no need for him to stick around. Liam seemed to have things under control. "Well, okay. Here's the paperwork, and here're his painkillers. From this bottle one every six hours; from this bottle, as needed, no more than six a day. And his antibiotics. Two pills twice a day, with meals. All the information is on the bottles, of course. And on the aftercare instructions, there…" Alex tried to point it out, but Liam wasn't looking at the pages.

"Got it," Liam said. "Thanks."

"He needs to keep taking the antibiotics until they're all gone, even if he doesn't think he has an infection."

"I know that. But thanks for the reminder."

"And his doctor's name… well, there's the contact info for his doctor back in New York," Alex said, pointing at the materials Liam was still ignoring. "But there's a doctor from the transplant team, too, and you should call him. Especially if Nick gets really groggy again. I mean, he's groggy now, but if it seems like he's getting worse, or if he can't wake up."

"Got it." Liam was pretty clearly getting impatient.

"And he might still be nauseated, so ease him into food gradually. Clear soup would be good. And then more later on, if he can keep the soup down. If he can't eat by tomorrow morning, call the doctor. He can ice the incisions if they feel hot or swollen. No baths for a couple days, but showers are fine." Alex wracked his brain, trying to remember other tidbits of information. It was all on the aftercare sheets, but he really didn't trust this Liam character to read them.

"Okay…" Liam said, and he started to move toward the door.

Alex had to force himself to follow. It felt wrong. He should be staying there with Nick, watching over him, protecting him. *He* could be trusted to get the medicines right; Liam couldn't.

But Liam was Nick's boyfriend. He was the one who had flown in from New York to help out. Alex was nothing. "Thanks for your time," Liam said as he opened the door.

"See you, Nick," Alex said quietly.

He hadn't really expected a reply, but Nick dragged his head up off the quilt and stared blearily in Alex's direction. "I feel like shit," he mumbled. "But thanks."

"You're giving me flashbacks to the mornings-after when we were kids," Alex said. "This is like ten bad hangovers rolled into one."

"And I didn't get to have any fun the night before." Nick squinted thoughtfully, then gave a slow, painful leer. "Well, I had a *little* fun…"

Was that something Nick felt he could mention in front of his boyfriend, or was he still stoned? Or was he just babbling, maybe not even thinking about the kiss in the elevator? Alex had no idea. "Feel better, Nick," he said quickly, and headed for the door.

Liam stepped aside to let him go, then shut the door firmly after him. Alex stood in the hallway and tried to put it all into perspective. When he'd woken up that morning, he'd genuinely expected to spend the whole day in the office. He'd somehow let himself be tempted to go to the hospital, then to stick around for most of the day, and finally to drag Nick's drugged-up ass back to his hotel to deliver him to his somewhat-hostile boyfriend. He wondered what had happened in the office while he was away, but he didn't care enough to call and find out.

Nick woke up slowly, and wished he could go back to sleep. His head hurt, and when he moved, his lower back flared with outraged pain. But he kept going. He'd been woken by the ringing of his phone, and while he didn't think he'd get to it before the call went to voice mail, it was a reminder that he had things to do. He stumbled across the room and found his phone, then looked at the "missed call" display on the screen. And then at the time. Quarter past nine. He'd slept in.

He looked over at Liam, who was still sound asleep, then hit the callback button. "Colin. What's up?" Nick's trusted colleague hadn't formally taken over the SeaCo CEO position yet, but he was doing most of the job while Blake transitioned to his new life. If he was calling, it probably wasn't just to say hello.

"We just got an interesting package couriered in," Colin said cautiously. "It looks clear enough, but I've got a few people reading it over."

"What are you talking about, Colin?"

"It's an offer on the SeaCo factory property. There are some conditions, but overall... it's offering almost 5% more than your bid."

"What?" Nick wished his head would stop pounding. "Are you serious?"

"I am."

"Is it from someone legit? Someone with the capital to back it up?"

"I think so, yeah. We're doing a little quick research on it, but Nick... it's from your father. Blake Colton just outbid you."

CHAPTER TWELVE

"Why?" Alex asked. "Do you have some actual plans for the land? Are you *interested* in real-estate development? And, honestly— you did it while Nick was in the hospital, donating bone marrow to your critically ill daughter?" Alex wasn't sure whether he was impressed or aghast at Blake's ruthlessness.

"He took over my company, my life's work, while I was preoccupied with that same little girl's health. This doesn't compare. If he wants the land badly enough he can bid again, and I'll have done nothing worse than raised the price and made a little bit more money for the SeaCo shareholders, the ungrateful bastards."

"And for yourself. If he outbids you, you'll have made money for yourself, by making Nick pay more."

"Whose side are you on, here?" The tone was light and joking, but Blake's eyes were intent. "You seem pretty interested in Nick's financial welfare all of a sudden. And you were pretty concerned about his physical state yesterday…"

"Someone had to be," Alex shot back. "His boyfriend was too busy preening to be at the hospital, and you ditched him as soon as you could. It would have been cruel to leave him there alone."

"And it's always your job to look out for Nick." Blake sat down in his big desk chair and looked at Alex appraisingly. "Do I need to be worrying about your loyalty? Do you think you've got a conflict of interest?"

Alex snorted bitterly. "Seems like you've already decided that; you didn't contact me about this bid, but you must have had someone look it over, right? Nick thought my loyalty was questionable, too. He fired me yesterday, right before the surgery. I no longer represent SeaCo Toys."

Blake squinted in disbelief. "And you still spent the day worrying about him and looking after him."

Alex decided not to mention that he'd even spent a bit of time making out with the son of a bitch. "He was right. It was a good business move."

"So's this," Blake said emphatically. "I've looked into it. Nick's bid was on the low end of fair for the land; mine's in the middle. If he's got any sense, he'll still overbid me. If he doesn't, then I've bought a good chunk of land at a good price. Either way, it's a win."

"And you have the capital to cover it?" They didn't generally discuss Blake's finances; Alex wasn't the man's accountant, so it wasn't his business. But Blake hadn't had any real income from SeaCo for years; how extensive were his other investments? How much money was left, after Blake had been living off his savings for so long?

"I'm fine," Blake said, just a little stuffily. "And what's going on with you and Marta? Helena wanted to invite the two of you for dinner; I told her not to, but she wants to know why."

In other words, don't ask about Blake's potential weakness unless you're prepared to have him tear yours wide open. "We're working on some things. There are... some issues."

"So fix them," Blake said firmly. "You have to work at relationships, Alex."

"We are." Well, that wasn't quite right. "Individually. We're thinking things over." He might as well lay a little groundwork for future revelations, he decided. "But it's pretty serious. I really don't think we're going to be able to work it out."

Blake made a face that suggested he was feeling annoyance more for himself than for Alex. "Because of whatever happened with Nick? Marta's a sensible girl. I can't imagine why you would have told her, but if you did, I'm sure she'll come around."

It felt odd to resist Blake's attempts to insinuate himself into Alex's personal life. Felt odd to resist Blake in any capacity, really. The lawyer/client relationship was just the latest iteration of the Díaz family working for Blake Colton, and the subservience sometimes felt like it was encoded in Alex's DNA. But the current conversation was well beyond the business sphere. "I appreciate your interest, but it's something we're going to have to work out on our own."

"Come on, Alex! She'll forgive you if you just crawl a little. Say you'll get therapy, or something."

The words Alex wanted to say were dancing around in his head, taunting him. *I don't think gay conversion therapy actually works, Blake. And I'm not looking to be cured, anyway.* But he didn't want to see Blake's expression after the words were out, and he didn't want any chance of the conversation getting back to his parents. He'd tell them, eventually. But until then, "At the very least, we're taking a break. So, no, dinner probably isn't a good idea." Alex stood up. He hadn't been invited to Blake's office, he realized, and it was a bit presumptuous to have just dropped by now that the man had moved his center of operations to his family home. Alex couldn't bill for the visit, so what the hell was he doing there? Was he being just as nosy as Blake had been? Everything was too convoluted, and Alex's head was starting to spin. "Obviously it's your decision about Nick and the land deal. And your decision about what lawyer you want. Is this just a one-time thing, or do you want me to send your files somewhere?"

Blake had the courtesy to look a little embarrassed. "I called Marta. You were busy, and I wanted to move fast. And Helena wanted to make sure she was okay."

"I'm sure she did a good job." The truth was, Marta had a much better eye for detail than he did. Alex knew what his firm's partners would want him to do next: he needed to wiggle himself back into Blake's good graces, saying whatever it took to ensure that SeaCo's next legal issue would be brought to him. The partners were already watching Alex closely, expecting him to make more of an effort to get new clients… and here he was, losing them instead. He knew he should fight, but he was just too tired. "You know how to reach me if you need to."

"I still want you to be my lawyer, Alex. Just not in situations that directly involve Nick. You understand."

He understood that his stupid infatuation had cost him his fiancée and was now threatening his career. "Like I said, you know how to reach me."

He let himself out of Blake's office and was almost to the front door when he heard a female voice calling his name. He turned to see Helena hurrying toward him. "I'm glad I caught you," she said.

"How's Adrianna doing?" he asked automatically. He'd asked Blake the same question when they'd greeted each other, but he knew Helena would have a different perspective than Blake's almost scientific report.

"Well, I think. She's still all tired out, but she's cheerful. Optimistic. She says she can feel the super-charged cells moving in."

"That's great. They're keeping her in the hospital, though?"

"Oh, yes. For another few weeks, at least. We're hoping for a day visit for Damon's birthday." She frowned. "And then we thought that might not be the right day; would she steal all the attention away from him?"

"Wait and see how she's feeling," Alex suggested. "No point in worrying about it yet."

"Good idea. Besides, I have to save some of my energy for worrying about you and Marta. What is this Blake is telling me about the two of you having trouble?"

Alex looked nervously around the foyer, hoping his mother wasn't nearby. "I haven't told my parents yet. I probably shouldn't have told Blake. Please keep it quiet, okay?"

"But what's gone wrong, Alex? Is there something we can do?"

"Nothing's wrong. It's just an adjustment."

"So you're working it out? Are you seeing a counselor, or anything?"

"No. We're…" But he couldn't get into it. Couldn't explain without saying something he shouldn't. "We've agreed not to discuss it with other people until we've figured a few things out."

Helena frowned. She was a take-charge woman and wasn't used to being thwarted, but she was also generally respectful of other people's privacy. It would have been fun to see the instincts at war if it had been someone else's business she was being asked to stay out of. As it was, he didn't want to stick around to see which side won. "I appreciate your concern, Helena," he said, and he escaped.

It was so clear what they wanted from him. And he'd managed to give it to them for so long. Now he was throwing it all away. It would have made sense, maybe, if he were sacrificing their happiness in order to achieve his own, but he didn't have that comfort to fall back on. He had no idea what he was doing, no interest in experimenting or trying to meet new people. He only wanted Nick, and Nick was taken. Was it really that important to express some obscure inner truth, or would it be better to just let things go back to the way they used to be?

"I think I may be stuck here a bit longer than I'd planned." It wasn't true, exactly, but Nick wasn't too worried about that. "And I know you're getting bored. I was thinking maybe you should head on to Hawaii without me. You're good at making friends; you'd be fine on your own. Or you're always saying that your sister doesn't get to travel much—do you want to see if she can join you? My treat." Nick watched Liam try to hide his thoughts. He was obviously tempted to take Nick up on the offer; shopping in Seattle wasn't that entertaining for someone used to New York, and Liam *did* love Hawaii. But Liam was always careful to maintain his relationship with Nick; he had a long-term plan and wasn't looking to throw that away for a quick payoff. "To be honest, I'm finding you more of a distraction than I'd expected." Nick let Liam take that as a compliment, even though the distraction had not generally been pleasant.

"I can't leave you alone, babe. You're still not feeling all that well. And that uptight creep who dropped you off yesterday? You can't count on him. He couldn't get rid of you fast enough! He acted like it grossed him out just to touch you—wouldn't even help you into the room!"

Nick didn't remember that, exactly, but he did remember Alex being impatient about the keycard. And Nick had definitely stumbled into the room on his own power, because he remembered thinking he might fall down and realizing there was no one to catch him. But none of that was important. Nick was getting rid of Liam because he was annoying, not because he was in the way of anything else. And maybe it was time to be clearer about that, because Nick was pretty sure he wasn't going to be calling the guy again once he got back to New York. "I'm feeling fine, Liam. But I'm not really fit for anything too strenuous, if you know what I mean. I appreciate your coming out here, and I hope you've had a good time. But I'm thinking of the Hawaii trip as a sort of goodbye gift, to be honest."

Liam stared at him a moment, eyes wide with surprise more than anything like hurt. It wasn't a good look on him. "What are you talking about? I flew all the way out here and now you're breaking up with me?"

"Well... yeah, if that's how you want to put it. I don't know that we were ever together, but if you want to call it breaking up, okay."

"No."

"I don't think that's an option, really."

"You're just tired." Liam had chosen his strategy, and he fluttered anxiously toward Nick as he put it into operation. "Does your head still hurt? And your back... I know you said you didn't want a massage, but I could focus on your shoulders and your legs, and leave out all the sore bits in the middle. You know you carry your tension in your shoulders! I can help you with that."

"I don't think I should keep taking free massages anymore, now that we're not... whatever."

Liam frowned at him. "We're friends, Nick. I care about you. You know that."

"And I appreciate it. We should keep in touch. But no more sex." No more payoffs, and wait and see how long Liam stayed interested in a friendship without bribes.

"I feel like you're rushing into this. You've just had a

traumatic experience, a brush with mortality! And you're still feeling crappy. It's not a good time to make a major decision, Nick." Liam smiled tenderly and put his hands on Nick's shoulders, then ran them down his chest. Nick caught them just before they hit his waistband.

"I need some space, Liam. You can book yourself a ticket to Hawaii, or back to New York. If you want, you can book a room somewhere else in Seattle for a while, but not at this hotel. I'd recommend against that option; we're done, and I don't think it's in your best interest to hang around and try to change my mind. But it's your call."

"You think you can ban me from this hotel?" Liam was apparently giving up on the possibility of salvaging this, and now the claws were coming out. "You don't own the hotel, Nick, and if we're not dating anymore, you have no say in where I stay!"

"I own my credit card, Liam. If you want me to pay, you need to go somewhere else. If you want to pay for your own room, obviously you can do that wherever you want."

"You're making a mistake! You think I don't know all your business secrets? Your deals? You talk about that stuff in front of me all the time! You think you can just throw me away and I'll go quietly?"

"You don't understand enough about any of it to even begin to know how to make trouble. But thanks for making the threat; it takes away any shred of guilt I might have been feeling about this." Nick smiled and turned toward the door. "I'm going out for a while; when I come back, you can either be gone, or you can let me know where you want to go and I can help arrange for you to get there." He turned the doorknob and looked over his shoulder. "Thanks again for coming. I'm sorry it didn't turn out the way you wanted."

He eased into the hallway and shut the door behind him, dialing his cell phone as he headed toward the elevator. He'd already checked with the credit-card company; they could temporarily lower his limit and refuse any charges beyond a certain ceiling. He'd activate that plan and arrange to have a new card overnighted to him. He'd give Liam a bit of a cushion, but only within reasonable limits. Getting taken to the cleaners wasn't part of the plan.

CHAPTER THIRTEEN

"The son of a bitch overbid me," Blake growled. His aggression was palpable, even over the phone.

But Alex had taken the opportunity to calm down the night before, and he had a new strategy for dealing with this. "I'm sorry you're upset about that," he said neutrally. "Has my mother mentioned the Memorial Day barbeque to you yet? She was wondering whether it would be better to set that as the goal for Adrianna's visit home from the hospital. It's a couple days before Damon's birthday, but if Anna can make it, we'd have a chance to celebrate her and still give Damon lots of attention on his day." He wasn't surprised by the silence, so after giving Blake a chance to respond he added, "It's our turn to host this year. I think Mom was going to speak to Helena and see if she wanted to switch years, or if she'd be okay bringing Anna to our house."

Another pause, and this time Alex waited it out. Finally, Blake said, "Why the hell are you talking about a barbeque? I just told you Nick overbid me on the SeaCo land."

"But you think I may have a conflict of interest. So I didn't think it would be good for us to talk about SeaCo." Alex wasn't quite sure where he was getting the balls from, but it felt pretty good to stand up for himself. "You called me, so it seemed rude to refuse to talk at all, and I thought the barbeque would be a good neutral topic."

"Is your mother planning to invite *Nick* to the barbeque? Are we allowed to talk about that?"

"We can talk about it, but I really have no idea. I don't think she is, but I haven't discussed it with her. I'm sure she'd be happy to speak to you about it."

"The little bastard is determined to win. He wants to make me look bad. You should see the message he sent to the SeaCo shareholders, gloating."

Well, so much for Alex's attempt to stay out of it. Blake was running hot and cold on the entire deal, sometimes trying to protect Nick, other times wanting to crucify him. The rapid attitude shifts probably weren't surprising, given all the stresses in the man's life, but it wasn't good for business. "I don't think anyone will think less of you for being outbid. The price must be getting pretty high, now. You did what you wanted: you drove the price up, to the shareholders' benefit. I don't see how that's a loss for you."

"He won't see it that way."

"Who cares how he sees it? You started this to keep him from running afoul of conflict of interest rules, right? It's become clear that he's taken precautions to avoid the potential issues; he's not as reckless as you thought. So there's no need to continue just to prove a point. This isn't a competition, it's business."

"You say shit like that, and you expect to make it as a corporate lawyer? Business is all about competition, Alex. You should know that by now."

And Blake should know to keep his emotions out of his decision making. He'd started out with reasonably good intentions, but his pride was obviously taking over. But Alex's courage had apparently run out, so he just hummed noncommittally into the phone. "Is there anything I can do for you, Blake? Marta started the deal, so she should handle the cleanup as well, if there is any. Do you need me for anything else?" Alex's desk wasn't exactly overflowing with work, but he didn't think Blake needed to know that.

"Be on standby," Blake ordered. "I'm not sure I'm done with this."

"You know where to find me. Say hi to Helena and the kids for me."

"Fine." Blake hung up, and Alex returned his own phone to its cradle. He'd barely gotten started on the contract he was supposed to be reviewing when the phone rang again, Blake's number on call display.

"Alex Díaz," he said into the handset.

"Who the hell is Liam Malloy?"

"Uh… I'm not sure. What's the context?"

"Somebody just called the house—the private line. He said he was Nick's boyfriend, got the number from him, and wanted to talk to me. What the hell is this about?"

"I have no idea." But he had to add, "I did meet a guy named Liam at Nick's hotel, when I dropped him off after the surgery. I think they're dating…"

"Why does he want to talk to me?"

To broker a truce? Was Liam that foolhardy? Or was he just more courageous than Alex? "I'm not sure."

"Did you know Nick was seeing someone?"

"I did after I met Liam in Nick's hotel room. Before that, no."

"Is this legit?"

"Blake, I have no idea. You could give Nick a call and see…" Alex knew he was wasting his breath.

"Let *him* call *me*," Blake said.

Alex couldn't help himself. "Is that what would get you talking? If I could convince Nick to give you a call, would you sit down with him? Would you at least try to stop this ridiculous competition? Because I know what you mean about business, but this isn't just business. It's family, and ego, and old hurts that have festered for too long. If you and Nick talked, you could start to clear the air."

"If he called me, if he *asked* me for a meeting, I'd see if I had time."

That was about all Alex had realistically expected. "Given that I'm not acting for you at the current time, would you see it as a conflict of interest if I approached Nick with that possibility?"

"You wouldn't give him any inside information?"

"I don't think I have any. Do I?"

"Probably not, no." Blake snorted. "You can spend your free time however you want to. But don't get your hopes up. Nick's a stubborn son of a bitch."

"I might not do it," Alex said quickly. The whole idea was stupid. "I mean, if I did, it would be for the family, not for business. And you're right, it probably wouldn't do any good."

"No, no... give it a try. Feel free."

And there it was, a tiny note of hope in Blake's voice, not quite drowned out by his ego and his stubbornness. He wanted things to be better with Nick, but he couldn't try to make it happen. He was too busy making it all worse. "Maybe," Alex said. "If I can find the opportunity."

"If it comes up," Blake agreed. "In the meantime, though... I might as well meet with this Liam Malloy, and see what he wants."

"Sure," Alex agreed. It was strange, but he couldn't see any harm in it.

Liam was gone. He'd been gone the night before when Nick came back from his walk, and he'd stayed away, which was more than Nick had really expected. Things seemed to be working out pretty well in that department.

And his bid had gone through that morning. He had to remember to keep his mouth shut around the SeaCo people, but he was being careful. He'd been planning this for a long time and he wanted it to go smoothly, with no allegations of impropriety. The simplest way to ensure that was to stay away from the place entirely, but without SeaCo business there wasn't a whole lot left to occupy his time. He was just sitting around, waiting to hear what happened with the real estate deal. Waiting for the next step.

So he went for another walk. He'd already ruined one pair of Italian dress shoes since coming to Seattle; the combination of puddles and extensive use was not kind to them. He should probably switch to running shoes and go for a jog, but that seemed a little too bouncy for his post-surgery body. He wasn't feeling sick anymore, but he wasn't exactly 100%, either. Walking was a good way to burn off some energy without stretching his healing wounds too much.

He didn't pay much attention to the route he was taking, but he wasn't particularly surprised when he found himself outside a tall, modern downtown apartment building. He knew the address; it was in his files. He should have kept walking, but instead he wandered inside, found the relevant number, and pushed the buzzer.

Alex sounded confused when he answered, and Nick tried to look non-psychotic as he looked up at the camera that was sending his image upstairs. "Nick?"

"Hi. Bad time?"

"Uh… no, I guess not."

Belatedly, Nick glanced at his watch. It was only seven o'clock. Still a civilized hour for paying surprise visits to estranged old friends. "I just wanted to say thanks," he said.

"You don't have to…" Alex started, then broke off and asked, "Do you want to come up?"

"If you're not busy."

The door buzzed as it unlocked. Nick went through and found his way to the elevator and when the doors slid open upstairs, he saw Alex waiting for him halfway down the hall. The view hit him harder than it should have, but it felt so right. Nick returning home. Alex there, happy to see him. They'd go inside and talk about their days, maybe have a couple glasses of wine, and then fall into bed. Sex, sure, but then they'd snuggle up together like when they were kids, their bodies so mingled that the only way to tell which limb belonged to which boy was the difference in skin tones.

But that had been a long time ago, and everything had changed. Nick kept his smile neutral as he walked down the long hallway.

"How'd you know where I live?" Alex asked as Nick drew closer. He didn't sound upset, just curious.

"Files," Nick said. "Your home address was on... I don't know, actually. But I saw it somewhere. Remembered it."

"Well, come on in," Alex said, and stepped aside to let Nick past.

"Thanks." Nick looked around, trying to find a trace of the boy he'd known in the clean, modern lines of the apartment. "Nice place."

"I guess. I'm hardly ever here." Alex looked temporarily abashed, and Nick had to guess about why.

"Because you're at work, or at your fiancée's," he said.

"Something like that."

"She's a lawyer, too, right?" It was a bit like picking a scab, but Nick honestly couldn't tell whose skin was underneath the injury.

"She is." Alex fixed his eyes on the windows that ran the length of the room on the far side. "But she isn't exactly my fiancée anymore."

Nick had no idea how to respond to that. "I'm sorry?"

Alex shook his head impatiently and started for the kitchen. "Do you want a drink?" He stopped, then said, "Just water or milk, I guess, if you don't want alcohol." He turned back and peered at Nick curiously. "Did you give up drinking?"

Nick shrugged. "Yeah. No big deal, but it was throwing me off my game. I didn't have money for it, at first, and then I needed to keep my head clear. So I gave it up."

"My treat, this time. Do you need to keep your head clear around me, or do you want a beer?"

Nick wanted to laugh. He had to keep his head clear around Alex most of all. "I'm fine, thanks. I could have some water, I guess, if you want."

"No," Alex said, coming back from the kitchen. "Would you like to sit down?"

The whole thing was awkward and stupid. Nick was in the middle of something big, business-wise, and Alex was a distraction at best. At worst, he could screw the whole thing up if Nick said the wrong thing to him. Still, Nick wanted to stay. He sank into the nearest armchair, then squinted at the rest of the furniture. "No pet hair," he said. "You always wanted pets. I guess apartments aren't ideal for dogs, but you don't have a cat? Or do you have one of those freakish hairless ones?"

Alex looked startled. "No. No pets. I'm not really home enough."

"Yeah. Shit's a bit trickier when you're grown up, huh?"

Alex squinted at him. "I'm trying to remember... I can't think of any dreams you had. Nothing to call you out on, and see if you got around to making the dream come true."

"No," Nick said slowly. "I didn't get around to it." His only dream, as far as he could recall, had involved spending every minute of his life with Alex.

Alex looked curious, but didn't pry. "They're pleased with Adrianna's progress. You did a good thing, there."

"I hope it works out. But that's what I wanted to thank you for. Getting me back to the hotel. I was a bit of a mess, as I recall."

"It was nothing. Glad to help. And I got to meet Liam." There was a definite question in Alex's voice, and Nick decided not to ignore it.

"Yeah, that must have been a treat for you. I needed someone to play nursemaid, and I thought he'd be better at it than he was. He's gone, now."

"Gone? Back to New York?"

"I don't know. I guess I could check my AmEx statement and see where the charges are coming from, but I don't really care that much." Too late, Nick remembered that Alex wasn't likely to be impressed by Nick's cavalier attitude, or by the way he'd disposed of an inconvenient bedmate. Alex looked like he was trying to figure something out. Probably nothing too complimentary to Nick. "What happened with you and the fiancée?"

Now Alex looked confused in a whole new way. "I made out

with you, Nick. I had to tell her about that. Understandably, she's upset. We're taking some time to think things over, but..."

Nick waited for Alex to finish. He really wanted to know how that sentence was going to end. But apparently Alex's mind had moved in a different direction. "You've never wavered? Never tried to be straight?"

Nick grinned. "I got that out of my system in high school." He tried to see this from Alex's perspective, but it wasn't easy. "Damn. You really should have fucked around more when you were a kid. Are you saying you're having trouble with her because you realized you were gay?"

"Something like that," Alex muttered.

"You've only been with women, since me?"

"Only with her," Alex said. He sounded miserable, now. "You, and then her. That's it. And now... I have no idea."

"Jesus, Alex. You are too hot to be that much of a loser." It wasn't the most sensitive thing Nick had ever said, but at least there was a compliment attached to the insult.

But Alex didn't seem interested in taking it. "Hot. Me. Yeah, right, Nick."

"Are you serious?" This was ridiculous. "You're smoking hot, Alex. You always have been. Your perfect skin, and your eyes are so big and brown, and you've got a really good build, like a gymnast or something. You could snag any guy you wanted, if you'd put even a little bit of effort into it. Any woman, too, I expect, though I'm not exactly an authority in that area."

"Not women," Alex said. He sounded like he couldn't decide whether to be amused, embarrassed, or fascinated by the conversation. "Men. I'm gay. I did a good job of hiding it, for way too long. But I'm gay."

"Yeah. I think we figured that out a long time ago, didn't we? I thought we established it pretty damn clearly."

"Well, then you took off. It was harder to be sure, without you around to remind me. I had to figure it out on my own."

"You did a really shitty job, Alex."

The laugh was half surprise, half amusement. "Yeah, I really did."

God, Nick wanted to touch him. His body knew exactly what to do, where they would fit together, how they would make each other feel. He tried to make his voice light as he said, "I feel like I should be taking you out to a gay bar or something. Show you the ropes, help you explore." He couldn't help letting his voice get a little heavier as he added, "But I don't want to do that. I don't want to let you out of this apartment. I don't want to share."

Alex's eyes were wide, and Nick wondered whether he'd gone too far. A couple of kisses weren't a huge deal, but Nick was suggesting they do a lot more, and Alex was obviously freaking out. Nick stayed as still as he could. He could almost hear Alex's heart pounding from across the narrow room. When Alex finally took a deep breath, Nick stood up slowly. "Do you want me to leave?" he asked.

Alex shook his head jerkily. "No," he squeaked.

"Do you want me to stay over here?" Nick held his breath as he waited for the answer.

Alex's eyes went back to their wide, round state, but he managed to say, "No."

Nick felt like an animal on the prowl. He wanted to pounce and bite and claim, but he forced himself to stalk at least a little longer. He stepped forward, stopped, and waited until Alex rose jerkily to his feet. Another step then, Nick's gaze locked on Alex's, and then one more. He was close enough to touch, now, but he kept his hands to himself. "I can still leave," he said softly. "If you think this is a mistake."

"It's a mistake," Alex agreed softly, but before Nick could move away, Alex was the one to pounce. He surged forward, one hand catching behind Nick's head, the other grabbing the front of his shirt, and pulled their bodies together while their mouths met in a fierce clash. Teeth more than tongues, nails attached to strong fingers dragging and clawing. Alex apparently hadn't had satisfying sex in a decade, and he'd obviously been saving up his desire.

It was almost overwhelming, but not quite, because underneath all the fierce need was *Alex*. Nick brought his hands up to the sides of Alex's head and held him still while he pulled his own face away for a moment. "Shhhh, Alex. Shhhh…" A gentle kiss to one cheekbone and then the other, and some of the desperation drained from Alex's warm brown eyes. "Whatever you want. I'm not going anywhere. We can do whatever you want."

Alex's body relaxed a little, and when he moved forward again Nick released his grip and let the kiss happen. It was a little slower now, deeper, and it felt absolutely right. The same mix of strange and familiar, Alex's tongue exploring and demanding as his hands tugged at Nick's clothes with only a little more control than before.

"Bedroom?" Nick suggested between kisses. "A bed would be good. Naked would be even better."

"Yeah," Alex breathed, and his fingers twined through Nick's, holding on desperately as if he thought Nick might try to escape. It was absurd, of course. Nick squeezed Alex's hand tight; there was nowhere else in the world he would rather be.

CHAPTER FOURTEEN

Alex's body hadn't felt like this since the last time he and Nick had been naked together. He allowed himself to get lost in the sensations; he didn't have to worry about whether he was doing things "right," didn't have to monitor his reactions or make sure his partner was pleased. Nick was in charge, and for all that Alex remembered their teenage sex as spectacular, Nick had obviously learned a few things in the intervening years.

Alex let out a gasping breath he hadn't known he was holding, and the exhalation pulled a thready whine from his throat. "Oh, God, Nick, please…"

Nick's mouth returned to view, curved into a self-satisfied smirk, but his hand stayed wrapped firmly around Alex's cock. "'Please' what? More?" and he tightened his grip, his fingers squeezing as they slid. It was just the right side of painful. "Or less?" and his hand loosened, then flattened and ran up over Alex's tense abs to gently tweak a nipple.

"I don't know," Alex gasped, and Nick's eyes softened as he leaned down for a deep, wet kiss. His body shifted over so it was half on top of Alex's, and the weight was exciting and comforting at the same time. Alex felt shielded and possessed, and Nick's confident explorations with hands and mouth reinforced it all. Nick knew what he was doing, and Nick would make Alex feel good. Just like he always had. How had Alex survived without this for over a decade?

"Nick," Alex moaned, and then a little louder, "*Nick*." He found the coordination to reach for Nick's head, twisting his fingers in the short hair and pulling Nick's mouth back to his. A quick kiss, then Nick looked Alex in the eyes and smiled in understanding.

"Okay," he said softly. He shifted a little more, lining their cocks up and wrapping his long fingers around both of them, creating a beautiful Nick-and-Alex channel. Sweat and pre-come made their cocks glide smoothly, and Nick rocked his hips just right, rubbing against Alex, grinding into him, and driving him, shuddering and gasping, over the edge into ecstasy.

Alex cried out and felt Nick's mouth there to greedily swallow the sounds. He drove his hips up and found Nick's body, warm and strong, waiting for him. And he almost collapsed as Nick urged him into another wave of pleasure, and another.

"Oh, God," he finally whispered, and Nick soothed him with a gentle kiss. It was too much. So many years of his life, without this. Why? Had Nick actually been bad for him? What would have happened if Alex hadn't turned away from the man he loved? If Nick hadn't left town, if Alex hadn't let himself be dragged into a nest of lies, if... So many ifs, and almost all of them seemed to lead to a world where Alex hadn't spent more than a decade as an empty shell. He felt his eyes stinging and sat up so quickly his forehead almost knocked Nick in the chin. He wanted to swing his legs over the side of the bed, maybe even walk away until he got himself back under control, but his body was still tangled with Nick's, and Nick wasn't letting him go.

"Hey, hey," Nick said gently. He wrapped an arm around Alex's shoulders and tried to pull him back, but Alex resisted. The tears were on his cheeks now, and he couldn't let Nick see that.

But he'd forgotten who he was dealing with. Nick was agile, and determined. Nick moved and was suddenly crouched on the floor in front of Alex, peering up at him with concern. "Alex..." he started, a question in his voice.

Alex twisted away. "It's nothing. I'm sorry. I'm an idiot." Nick hadn't even come yet. This wasn't ridiculous post-sex emotion, it was insane during-sex emotion, and it was probably the least-cool thing Alex had ever done in his life.

"You're not an idiot. It's not nothing. And don't be sorry." Nick shifted again, returning to his spot behind Alex on the bed, and his arm wrapped back around Alex's chest as if it were the most natural thing in the world. "You always were wound a little tight. It's that passionate Latino blood, probably. My cool Nordic blood lets me be in control of my emotions; some people, looking at my immediate ancestry, might wonder whether we actually *have* any emotions to worry about." He kissed Alex's shoulder, then gave it a playful nip. "But you, you're sensitive. Like a delicate hothouse flower, ripped from your tropical home and forced to adapt to cold northern climes. Let your exotic nature free…"

Nick probably had more nonsense to share, but it was hard for him to keep talking after Alex spun around, pushed him onto his back, and kissed him. Alex could taste his own tears, which meant Nick probably noticed them too, but it didn't matter anymore. This was *Nick.* Old, funny, gentle Nick who had been with Alex through all the upheavals of their young lives. He pulled away just long enough to enjoy the view. Nick's smiling face, his pale golden skin, a little more hair on his chest than there used to be, defined abs, and then… Fuck! Alex was really, really bad at this. "I forgot all about you!" he gasped, staring at Nick's hard, beautiful cock.

"It's probably not too late to make it up to me…"

Alex was suddenly nervous. Nick had moved on, taken who-knew-how-many lovers, learned and grown and developed his technique. Alex hadn't seen a cock other than his own for more than ten years.

Nick was watching him thoughtfully, and his smile was sweet. "Just kiss me, then," he suggested, sliding his own hand downwards.

"No!" Alex protested, catching Nick's wrist and wrapping their fingers together. "I want to." And he did, he realized. He wanted to taste, and to feel the power of Nick's body. He kept his grip on Nick's hand and slid down the bed, kissing random spots as he went. Another wave of nerves when he reached his target, but when he gave the head a gentle kiss, Nick's fingers tightened around his in appreciation. Okay. This wasn't new. It had been a long time, but Alex could do this. He wanted to do it. A long lick from the base to the tip… that had felt good when Nick did it to Alex. But the real prize was still waiting, and Alex was ready to claim it. He wrapped his lips around the head, slid down the hard shaft as far as he could go, and promptly gagged. He pulled back, but somehow something had gone wrong, and now he was choking. On his own saliva? Was he that pathetic?

Nick had propped himself up on one elbow and was staring

down at him in amused concern. "You okay? Jesus, Alex, you weren't even that far down."

"I'm fine," Alex gasped between fits of coughing. "Just a second."

"Hand job would be fine, if this is too much for you."

"I can do it! Just give me a second."

"'Yeah, I choked him with my massive dick,'" Nick said with a grin. "That's what I'll tell all the boys."

That distracted Alex from his coughing, at least. "What boys?" He could hear the apprehension in his voice.

"What? Oh. No boys, I guess. I was just kidding."

"Yeah," Alex said. He needed to be cool. But… "I'm not… you know. Out. I haven't told my parents about this."

"You told your parents 'about this' a long time ago, Alex." Nick sounded impatient.

"That was last time. I need to… I need to do it my way. Please don't tell anyone, Nick."

"Your way? I pushed you out of the closet last time, and as soon as I left town you crawled right back in. I don't really think you *have* a way, do you?" The playfulness was gone. Apparently Nick would tolerate some types of weakness from Alex, but not others.

"Things are more complicated when you actually *care* about people, you know." The words were unnecessarily harsh. Despite being left hanging—again—Nick had seemed more disappointed than angry, yet now Alex was picking a fight. It made no sense, but he didn't seem to be able to stop. "You pushed me out of the closet, that's true. And then you ran away and left me to deal with the repercussions all by myself!"

"You broke up with me, Alex. I pushed you out of the closet, and you pushed me out of the relationship altogether. At least I had the guts to *stay* out."

"You 'had the guts'? You think hiding away like a spoiled little boy shows *guts*? Seriously?"

They both jumped when a tone sounded from the bedside table. Alex's phone. Two minutes ago he might not even have noticed it, but now... now it seemed like it might be a good distraction. He answered before his mind registered the name on the display.

"Marta?" he said cautiously.

"Hi." Marta sounded tense, but determined to be civil. "I need to talk to you."

"Now? It's not a great time."

"Not about that." Marta's impatience was uncharacteristic. "I'm calling you to request some documents. Okay? I'm not breaching client confidentiality."

"Okay..." Alex had no idea what was going on. "What do you need?"

Marta's voice was tight and careful. "I need all paperwork related to Blake Colton's ownership of his SeaCo shares. Whatever I'll need to allow him to buy some real estate on margin, using his SeaCo shares as collateral."

It was a moment before Alex could answer. "He wouldn't," he breathed. "Those are... he's always said those are for his children."

"I can neither confirm nor deny my client's intentions," Marta said carefully. "But I need those papers."

"They're with the accountant," Alex said absently. His mind was racing. "Blake knows that." Which meant Blake hadn't told Marta to call Alex, but she'd decided to do it anyway. Maybe because she didn't know where the papers were, or maybe because she thought Alex could do something about this. "He won't listen to me, Marta. I can't change his mind."

"Are you sure?" She paused, but he had no answer, so she continued. "Okay, then. I'll call the accountant. Sorry for disturbing you."

"No problem," Alex said out of habit. In fact, he mused as he disconnected the call, it was a huge damned problem. One caused by the man lying beside him on the bed. Only Nick wasn't lying there anymore, Alex realized as he turned around. He was sitting up, his

feet dangling off the far side of the mattress, and Alex saw his lower
back for the first time, the bruises and the four slit-like needle marks.
Nick wasn't even at full strength and he'd still been able to give Alex
a better orgasm than he could ever remember having. And then Alex
had mangled a simple blowjob and taken a phone call from his
maybe-ex-fiancée, telling secrets about Nick's father. For all that Nick
was trying to look casual, he couldn't have missed overhearing Alex's
side of the conversation. What had he said? He tried to remember
which words had been his and which had been Marta's.

"I should probably go," Nick said. There was no warmth in his
voice, but no anger, either. If anything, he sounded awkward.
"Sounds like you've got some work to do?"

"I don't know." No formal work; Alex didn't represent Blake
or SeaCo anymore; this was none of his business, professionally. But
personally? "I guess so. I have to go see…"

He paused, and Nick raised his hands. "It's cool. You've got
business." He'd apparently put his underwear on at some point
during the phone call, and he kept his back turned as he pulled on the
rest of his clothes. It was the practiced routine of someone used to
smooth escapes after sex, Alex realized. Nick hadn't come, but he was
clearly ready to go.

It hurt more than Alex wanted to admit, and he had no one to
blame but himself. He'd been bad at sex, he'd gotten paranoid and
freaked out, and he'd been an asshole. Of course Nick wanted to
leave, and Alex was humiliated enough already; he wasn't going to
beg. "Well, thanks for dropping by," he said as casually as he could
manage. He tried not to think about Nick pulling fabric over skin
dampened with sweat and Alex's come. Too dirty, too intimate.

"Thanks for helping out after the hospital," Nick replied
politely.

And that was it. Nick's erection was dying down, only visible
because Alex was looking for it, and he pulled on his shoes and
walked easily to the front door. Alex trailed along behind him, sheet
wrapped demurely around his waist, but there was no goodbye kiss,
no promise or even suggestion of future contact. Just a forced smile, a
quick wave, and the door shutting in Alex's face.

Alex wanted to cry again. He'd had everything he wanted again, but for such a short time. Apparently he was destined to make everything hard for himself, instead of just enjoying the moment.

Yeah, he wanted to cry, and that made him think of Nick's teasing, and that made him want to cry even more. But he wasn't a delicate hothouse flower. He wouldn't give in. He'd get things done, instead.

He dropped the sheet on the way to the bathroom. He needed a shower. Everything would be better once he washed away the evidence. He'd shower, change his sheets, and go to sleep. In the morning, he'd call Blake and see if there was any way to calm him down. Alex didn't think he'd succeed, but he should make the effort. If nothing else, it would help distract him from the memories of Nick's strong hands, soft lips, and gentle smile. Alex needed to forget about all that and focus on the things he could control.

CHAPTER FIFTEEN

Nick was getting tired of doing stupid things. He never should have gone to Alex's apartment, and he *absolutely* shouldn't have touched the guy. The fiancée calling had made that crystal clear. Nick had charged into Alex's well-ordered life, turning things upside down with no thought for the repercussions of his actions. He was doing the same thing Blake had accused him of all those years ago, and it wasn't fair. At least he'd managed to get out of the apartment before Alex let any more information about the deal slip out; Nick wanted to keep the transactions clean for Alex's sake as well as his own. A young lawyer couldn't afford to have allegations of impropriety leveled against him.

Nick needed to keep his mind on business. He needed to stay the hell away from Alex, and from everyone else associated with his old life. He knew that, and yet the next morning he got ready for work, started walking, and ended up at the hospital where Adrianna was. Maybe he needed to stop walking everywhere; he could probably trust a cab driver to get him to his intended destination, and he obviously couldn't trust himself.

Still, he was there. And Adrianna *was* his half-sister. Alex was off-limits, but Adrianna was just a little girl. What harm could she do him?

Wait. He hadn't left Alex's because *he* was worried about getting hurt; he'd been trying not to interfere in Alex's life. So going to see Adrianna was fine. She didn't have a stable life for him to disrupt; hell, for her, he was probably a source of stability. Not to mention bone marrow.

So he went to the front desk and asked if Adrianna Colton was still in the same room.

"She's in 2212," the woman behind the counter said after checking a computer screen. "But she's on restricted visitation." She peered up at Nick as if trying to figure out who he was. "Are you a member of her immediate family?"

That shouldn't have been a tricky question. "Uh… no. Not really."

"Sorry," the woman said with an efficient smile. "They're trying to minimize exposure to germs."

Nick supposed he could have argued. The little girl was currently sharing his bone marrow, so probably sharing a little air wouldn't hurt her. But there wasn't any pressing need to see her, and he sure didn't want to carry in any infections. "Okay. I'll find something at the gift shop for them to send up and let her know I came by."

"She may not be able to have toys, if they can't be properly sterilized. The staff will definitely let her know you were here, though."

"Thanks," Nick said. He felt deflated, and oddly angry with himself. He hadn't even really *wanted* to see the kid, and now he was disappointed that he couldn't go upstairs? It was stupid.

He was in the gift shop, trying to figure out what could be sterilized that a little girl would still like, when he heard someone saying his name. A woman's voice, soft and lightly accented. Recognition gave him time to collect himself before he turned around. "Rosa," he said with a polite smile. "It's good to see you. How've you been?" Then he frowned. "I hope you're not here to see Adrianna. I already tried, and they said visits were for immediate family only."

"I just came from her room," Rosa said. She looked at him as if she couldn't decide whether to be sad or angry. "They call me her aunt."

"Aunts are immediate family?"

"Family is whoever we *say* family is, Nicky." She seemed to have settled on being sad. "You haven't learned that yet?"

He really didn't think he needed to listen to that from her. "I used to believe that, but it turns out that we don't always get to choose." He grabbed the nearest stuffed horse and headed for the cash register. "Good to see you," he said over his shoulder.

He knew she was staring at him as he gave the cashier Adrianna's room number, but he refused to turn around. He was a grown man and he wasn't going to be lectured by an aging housekeeper or anyone else. But on his way toward the door, when she said, "Nick, stop," he did. She'd been the only person who ever disciplined him as a child, more through disappointed looks than by actual punishments, and apparently the effect had lasted. He was still conditioned to obey.

"What do you need, Rosa?" he asked as offhandedly as he could.

"We should talk."

Nick was almost sure they shouldn't. "I was just heading to work. But I can give you my cell number, if you want, and you can call me later."

"No. We should talk now." She crossed the floor as confidently as a queen, looking up at him as she linked her hand through his arm. Nick remembered her standing just the same way in a photo taken at his high-school graduation, only then her face had been glowing with pride. "The cafeteria shouldn't be too busy at this time of day." She started walking, and it was impossible to resist.

Nick let himself be led through the lobby and down a short hall to the cafeteria, then inside and to a remote table by the windows. Only then did he balk. "This really isn't the best time."

"Sit down, Nicky."

He sat, damn it.

She looked at him for longer than was comfortable before saying, "You helped Adrianna. She's a sweet girl, and you did a good thing." It didn't sound like praise, exactly, just a statement of fact. Rosa leaned back in her chair and waved a casual hand through the air. "And you and your father… I can't worry about that. Mr. Colton has been good to me and my family, but his business is for him. He's never invited me in, and I've never wanted to visit." Fair enough. "What you did to me—leaving like that, and not coming back. I forgive you, even though you haven't asked me to. I loved you almost like my own, and you left me and frightened me. But you're forgiven." Nick wasn't sure he was *quite* forgiven, judging by her tone of voice, but he didn't think he wanted to argue about it. Especially not when he could tell she was building up to something bigger.

"How it affected Alex when you left, that's…" She shook her head at him and sighed. "I suppose that's not my business, either, but I want you to know. It broke his heart, Nick. He was so lost, for so long."

"Hang on. What did Alex tell you about it?" Nick didn't want to bust Alex on some long-ago lie, but he also didn't want to take the blame for something that wasn't his fault. "Because *he* dumped *me*, Rosa. I never would have left him. Not ever. But he said I wasn't good for him. He said I was *hurting* him." Nick had never said the words out loud before, but he'd replayed them in his mind too many times over the years. There was no doubting his recollection. "That's why I left."

She nodded sadly. "I know. That's why I wanted to talk to you, Nicky. I wanted to apologize."

"Wait. What?"

Another sad look, and she leaned forward and reached across the table to rest her hand gently on his forearm. "I'm sorry. He told you that because I told him he should. Because I thought it would be better for *both* of you to spend some time apart."

It wasn't as if Nick hadn't suspected that Alex's parents had been part of the decision. And it wasn't as if he really wanted to think about that terrible day any more than he had to. Still, it was hard to let go of this. "He must have agreed," he said. "He didn't do *everything* you guys said. He'd stand up for himself when he had to."

"Because of you," Rosa said softly. "He was strong because of you. You gave him the courage to take chances. But I told him it was good for *you*, not just good for him. If it had just been about him, I don't know what he'd have done. But I told him I was worried about you, and your father was worried about you. I said the two of you weren't good together."

"We were *great* together." It was pointless, a decade after the fact, but it seemed important that there be no doubt in anyone's mind about this.

And Rosa didn't argue. "I know. I thought you were making Alex reckless, making him do stupid things." She gave him a look. "And you were. Those silly stunts you came up with… Alex shouldn't have been doing any of that." A conciliatory pat on his arm. "But you were also helping him to *live*. To have adventures, and enjoy each day. Since you left, it's like he's just been going through the motions. I told him *you* were the one who was adrift, but it turns out that it was Alex all along. Without you, he does whatever anyone wants him to do. Practice corporate law, get engaged, be the dutiful son, look after his brothers and sisters." She smiled. "I know, it sounds crazy for a mother to be complaining about any of that. And I wouldn't be complaining if it made him happy. But it doesn't. And being happy is the most important thing."

"Maybe he was doing whatever *I* wanted him to, before. He's just a selfless person."

"I used to hear you two fighting all the time. Squabbling, mostly, but real fights sometimes. He wasn't just going along with you, Nicky. He cared about you, and he cared about other things, too, and he'd fight for what he believed in. Now?" She shrugged. "He drifts."

"He's gay." Completely inappropriate for Nick to say to Alex's mother, but the conversation had gone plenty of other weird places, so why not this one? "He's been pretending to be straight. I have no idea why he thought that was a good idea, but I imagine it would be pretty hard to pretend to care about a fiancée you don't actually want to marry."

She looked like she was thinking about arguing. Thankfully, after a moment she nodded. "I imagine it would be." And apparently that was all she had to say on the topic.

"What do you want from me, Rosa? Why are you telling me all this?"

Good questions, it seemed, because she took her time answering. "I don't know. You've been gone so long, Nick, and we have no idea what your life is like now. I've heard talk of a boyfriend;

I don't know how serious that is. I don't know if what you had with Alejandro is gone forever, and I don't know if you'd want it back even if you *could* have it." She pulled her hand back into her lap and straightened her shoulders. "But I wanted to apologize. I was part of destroying something beautiful. I did something that hurt my son, and hurt you. I'm sorry."

Nick had no idea what to say. Was all this true? Had he given up too soon? He'd been so determined not to hurt Alex, but maybe he'd done it anyway. He'd certainly hurt himself. "It was a long time ago," he managed. "I'm sure we've both gotten over it."

But Rosa shook her head. "I don't think Alex has. Have you?"

Nick jerked to his feet before he was even aware he was planning to stand. "It was good to see you, Rosa. I hope Adrianna does well. Please give her my best."

And that was all he could come up with. He forced himself to walk to the exit rather than jogging, thankful that she didn't try to stop him. He didn't turn around, didn't slow down until he was out of the building and halfway down the block. He had spent so much time thinking he shouldn't have come back to Seattle; it was frightening to think maybe he never should have left.

CHAPTER SIXTEEN

Alex hadn't really expected to be able to change Blake's mind, but he'd been surprised by the hostility with which the older man had greeted the attempt. "You've always had a blind spot with Nick," Blake said. "When you were a boy, it was worrisome but kind of cute. It's not cute anymore, Alex. You need to pick a side. And you know you can't count on him to stick around, so if you're smart, you'll pick my side. I'm the one who's always been there for you." Blake scowled disapprovingly as he added, "Years of working together, Alex. That should mean something to you."

"It does!" he'd protested. But he'd also remembered the nineteen years of friendship with Nick he'd thrown away, and wondered why Blake expected his own claim to get more respect. The first six years Nick had been away, Alex was in school; he hadn't been Blake's lawyer for all that long. Sure, SeaCo was one of the reasons Alex had been able to get a job at one of the most prestigious firms in town, but he no longer worked for SeaCo. Besides, all those years ago Alex had betrayed Nick's friendship as soon as it became inconvenient—why was Blake so sure Alex wouldn't do the same to him?

Almost a week later, Alex was still asking himself that question. He hadn't seen Nick since that beautiful, disastrous night, so maybe Blake had been right about Alex's loyalty. Or maybe Alex had just been too much of a coward to get in touch with Nick and risk another rejection.

Now, as he rang the doorbell of the Colton home, he wondered why he'd been summoned. Helena had called him, not Blake, but there hadn't been much point in asking her for details. She occasionally played secretary, but she wasn't really involved in Blake's business matters.

And neither was Alex, anymore. Actually, it was a relief to be out of the game. He'd seen the land sale mentioned in the business pages; it looked like Blake had won the bidding war, although no final price had been stated in the article. Maybe Blake had decided to bring Alex back into the loop for the development phase of the project. It probably wasn't a good sign for his future in corporate law that the thought evoked dread rather than excitement.

He expected to see his mother answering the door in the middle of the day, but instead it was Helena who pulled it open and stepped half-outside in her eagerness to give him a hug. "You're here!" She made it sound as if Alex offered some sort of salvation.

"I am. What's going on?"

"I don't know." Helena looked close to tears; it was an expression he'd seen far too often as she struggled to cope with Adrianna's illness. But he'd heard from his mother the night before that the girl was doing well, and it wouldn't make sense to call him to the house for a medical issue, so he waited for Helena to continue. She sighed and glanced almost furtively in the direction of her husband's office. "He won't tell me. But something's gone wrong, I can tell. With the business? With the land deal? I don't know."

"You think he'll tell me when he won't even tell you? Blake's not my biggest fan these days, you know."

"Yes, he is." She sounded absolutely convinced. "And he needs you. You know how old-fashioned he can be; he doesn't want to worry me, *and* he thinks I shouldn't bother my pretty little head with these things." Her snort didn't sound like it came from a head that was either pretty or little. "I'll have that fight with him—again— another day. For now, I just want to know what's going on. With you here, maybe he'll talk to us. Together."

It seemed like a long shot, but Alex let Helena guide him down the hallway to the familiar office door. As children, he and Nick had hidden on the staircase and done surveillance of this spot, fascinated by the forbidden sanctum. Now, Alex felt a little of the same anxious fascination as he lifted his hand and knocked tentatively on the heavy oak. "Blake?" he called softly. "It's Alex."

There was a pause, then a muffled response that Alex chose to interpret as "Come in."

He raised his eyebrows at Helena, took a deep breath, and pushed the door open.

Blake was sitting at his desk by the big bay window, as he so often did. He looked a little tired, maybe, his usual crisp tailoring slightly disheveled, but nothing too alarming. He looked up as Alex and Helena approached, and then his eyes darted back to the computer screen in front of him. Then back to Alex, and again to his wife before returning to the screen, and now it was clear something was wrong.

"What's going on?" Alex asked softly.

"You haven't heard? Your broker hasn't called you?"

"My broker? I don't... Oh, I just use an online system. I don't have that much in the market. What is it?"

Blake looked like he was going to refuse to answer, but apparently realized he'd already given too much away. He looked at Helena and said, "Maybe you could wait outside?"

"No." That was all, but the wordless communication between them was powerful. Blake was almost pleading with her, but Helena stayed firm.

Finally, Blake gave in. "SeaCo," he said raggedly. "The stock's plummeting. Down 15% this morning alone. There's no reason for it! It spiked with the real estate deal—people were excited about... about how much I paid." He sounded almost embarrassed about that.

"Well, it'll come back up," Alex said. He had no idea why the stock had fallen, but market fluctuations could be hard to predict. "You weren't looking to sell it anyway, were you? Hell, maybe it's a good time to buy... do you have any capital lying around?"

Blake's eyes were haunted as he raised them to Alex. "I'm in debt up to my eyeballs. I couldn't raise another cent if my life depended on it."

That confirmed an unpleasant suspicion. Blake had overextended himself trying to buy the SeaCo real estate. Still, this didn't sound all that problematic. "So a lost opportunity, then." He stopped. Blake wasn't stupid, and he wasn't over-emotional. If he was this upset, there was something more behind it. "What else?"

Blake clearly didn't want to answer, especially in front of his wife, but finally he said, "The land. My land, that I paid… that I paid too much for. It was Nick's fault! He sent his boyfriend here to give me false information! The little bastard told me Nick had development permits already lined up. He said Nick was willing to pay up to 20% more than his last bid! He said Nick had broken up with him, and he wanted to make him regret it!"

"But that wasn't true?" Alex didn't want to follow the path his mind was going down.

"Twenty percent more? Nick didn't overbid me at all! I was trying to drive the price up again, but the son of a bitch just stepped back and let the sale go through." Blake still seemed amazed by it. "I figured I'd be okay, because the land was ready to be developed. I'd just flip it, maybe take a bit of a loss, but no big deal." He shook his head in disbelief. "But now there's a fucking inquiry going on, some historical group claiming the building should have landmark status… They're going to get in the way of everything. There are no permits, and there never will be, not if they get their way! This should have come up before the bids; SeaCo was hiding it from me!"

"Maybe they hid it in plain sight," Alex said slowly. "You had Marta draw up the contracts on this, but you didn't give her time to do much research. Did SeaCo send over boxes of documents for you to review?" He could see from Blake's stunned expression that they had. "And you didn't have time to look through it all. You assumed Nick would know about it, and since he wanted the property, it must all be fine."

Blake looked shaken. "He *should* have known. Why the hell did he still want the land?"

"I don't think he did." Alex sank into the chair opposite Blake's. "From what I've seen of Nick, if he wants something, he gets it. And he didn't get the land. So… maybe he never really wanted it. Maybe the game you were playing with him, driving up the price, taunting him into overbidding… maybe he was playing the same game with you." *And he won*, Alex thought. But there was no point in saying it out loud. He sighed. "What if the stock price is falling because Nick sold his shares? He got you to overpay for the land, driving the price up. The stocks rose in response, and he took his profits and ran." It made sense. From the research Alex had been able to do on Nick's past business transactions, it made perfect sense. "Nick doesn't run businesses. Not long-term. He's certainly never been involved in real-estate development. He's a raider. He finds weak companies and buys cheap stock, then props the business up long enough to sell the stock at a higher price."

"You're saying this was a setup? He'd do that to his own father?"

Alex wasn't sure what to say to that, and Blake frowned at him, then looked back at the computer screen. "Of course he would," Blake said, as much to himself as to Alex or Helena. "I was willing to do it to him. He learned something from me, after all."

It hurt to see the confident man so cowed. "It's not that bad, is it? I mean, we can deal with the heritage designation if we have to. We can challenge it, or work around it. It's not like the land is useless. And the stock will bounce back. Some shareholders have panicked, probably, seeing the drop, but they'll come back, or new buyers will find it. The company itself is moving in a good direction."

"I bought the land on margin," Blake confessed, bitter at his own stupidity. "I used the SeaCo shares as collateral. My broker's already called once; I don't think they're going to give me much more time."

"More time?" Helena frowned in confusion. Alex wished he could claim the same ignorance, but he knew all too well what Blake was saying.

Blake waved a hand tiredly as if he couldn't find the energy to explain, so Alex turned to Helena. "A margin call. They loaned him the money with the shares as collateral, but the shares have to maintain a certain value or the brokerage can call in a portion of the loan." He looked at Blake, not wanting to confirm his suspicion. "If Blake can't repay the loan from his cash reserves or by selling something else, he'll need to sell some of the SeaCo stock to pay the brokerage."

Blake's voice was emotionless. "And when I sell, that will drive the price of the stock lower. Which will mean I still won't have enough collateral to cover what's left of the loan, which will mean another margin call. I'll have to sell more stock to repay more of the loan."

"And when you sell that stock, it will drive the price even further down." Helena stared at him as if she couldn't believe what she was hearing. "And you'll have to repay, so you'll have to sell more, and then…"

Blake was still staring at the computer screen, and Alex shifted around enough to see that it was a real-time stock-quote page. "And then it'll be over," Blake said quietly. "I'll have lost the final shares in the company my great-grandfather started over a hundred years ago. And I may still owe more money after that. I paid… I paid far too much for the land. But there should be *something* left for the family. I hope."

Alex swallowed through a throat gone dry, and he watched Helena as she stood up and walked behind the desk. She wrapped her arms around her husband's shoulders and kissed the side of his head. "We'll be fine," she said. "The money isn't important. We have each other, and the children. Adrianna is doing well. That's our blessing, our miracle. Nothing else matters."

Adrianna was doing well because of Nick's contribution. Was the family fortune the price to be paid for his benevolence? But Nick had never asked for anything like that. Besides, he must have been planning this for years, from before Adrianna got sick, maybe before she was even born. In business Nick was brutal and ruthless, and he didn't seem to care who got hurt. But on the personal side… he'd been afraid of the anesthetic, bothered by the entire process, but he'd gone ahead without complaining. The personal side of Nick was still kind.

Alex stood abruptly. Blake and Helena looked at him in surprise and he said, "Hold them off. The brokers. Tell them you've got something in mind."

"I've already tried that," Blake said tiredly.

"Well… sell as little as you can, then."

"Might be better to get it over with," Blake replied. "I can sell it all now for its current price, or sell it later for less."

Alex stopped walking and turned back toward the desk. "Yeah. Fine." He shook his head. He couldn't believe he was going to do this, but apparently he was. "Be a pussy, if that's all you've got left. Give up. But let me know now, so I don't waste my time and energy trying to find a solution." He paused to let Blake get over his shock, then lifted an eyebrow. "If you want to fight, I'll do everything I can to help you win. But if you're going to give up… yeah, you might as well get it over with."

"Do you have an actual plan?" Blake sounded as if he were afraid even to hope.

"Yeah." Alex grinned quickly. "Kind of."

"That's not too reassuring," Blake muttered. But he had at least a weak version of his usual expression, a hint of the cool, assessing look that had always made him so intimidating. "Okay. Go. Do what you can, and let me know how I can help."

"Absolutely." Alex didn't look behind him, and he broke into a jog as he headed down the familiar hallway. The plan wasn't much, but the first step was clear. He had to find Nick.

CHAPTER SEVENTEEN

Nick knew he should be celebrating. He'd followed his plan, achieved his goal, made a significant profit... everything he'd had in mind. He leaned back and looked at the numbers on the computer screen in front of him. It wasn't his biggest deal ever, but it was his fastest turnaround, and his highest percentage return on his initial investment. It was a victory. Getting to teach his father a lesson was just gravy.

Maybe he was dissatisfied because it didn't seem real yet. Everything had been so weird since his return to Seattle; he'd felt disjointed, sometimes like the boy who'd left all those years ago, sometimes like the man he was now. As a teenager he wouldn't have given a shit about a bunch of numbers on a computer screen. Maybe he should go to the bank and get it all in cash as a visual aid. Or maybe he should grow up and stop expecting a tidal wave of happiness all the time. Maybe this temporary reprieve from restlessness was the only victory celebration he could ever expect.

The knock at the door of his suite was a welcome distraction, especially after he saw who was outside. He'd been trying not to think about Alex, but it hadn't been working too well. And the deal was done, now. No more conflict of interest to worry about. Plus, Rosa's words had been dancing through his head all week. He smiled as he opened the door, but Alex responded with an agitated frown.

"What the hell are you doing, Nick? Or—*why* are you doing it?"

So, not the reunion Nick had been hoping for. But he stepped to the side and let Alex pace into the room.

"Is it deliberate? Do you *want* to ruin him, or do you just not care?"

It still hurt. That was the stupid part. After so long and with a lot of growing up, Nick should have been over it. But it still hurt to hear Alex sticking up for Blake instead of him. Nick shut the door and leaned against the wall. "I assume you're talking about my father?"

"You know who I'm talking about! You know what you did. Did you know he might lose everything? He's sitting right now in the house where he raised you, trying to convince his brokers to give him a little more time before they make a margin call."

Nick smiled sadly. "The house where *he* raised me? The house where he raised *you*, maybe. We both know your mom did a lot more to raise me than he ever did."

"Oh, the poor little rich boy. It was so sad, the way he paid for everything you wanted. So terrible of him to actually get *help* running his household. He sure does need to be punished."

"You're pushing it, Alex."

Alex stared at him in disbelief. "*I'm* pushing it? Are you a psychopath? Is that it? No feelings, no guilt… just greed."

Nick felt the familiar resentment and anger washing over him. "Greed? Me? Have you asked yourself how Blake got in trouble, Alex?" He pulled himself away from the wall and stepped closer. Alex backed away, but kept his eyes locked on Nick's. "He couldn't accept that he'd lost control of the company. Even though I didn't cost him a penny, he decided to do something he thought would cost *me* a fortune. He overbid me *twice* trying to jack up the price of that land. If he'd walked away, he'd have been fine. But he couldn't do that. And now you're asking me to feel guilty for playing the same game he was playing? Just because I won?" Nick shook his head. "Fuck that." More importantly, "And fuck you for coming here. For…" He stopped when he realized he wasn't sure he could control his voice. *Fuck you for caring more about his opinion than about me. Again.*

Alex's eyes were so wide that Nick wondered for a moment whether he'd actually said the words out loud. "That's not why I came here," Alex finally said. "When I left Blake's house, I was…" He shook his head. "I was going to appeal to your humanity. Your kinder side. I was going to ask you to help him, the way you helped Adrianna." He looked confused. "Somehow it came out wrong. I guess I got worked up on the way over. I don't know…"

"Old habits are hard to break." Nick made sure the sympathy in his voice was laced with sarcasm. "You worship the old man, you think I'm a loser—I get it. No big thing. But at some point you're going to have to realize who the real loser is, here. You're going to have to remember who *won*."

"Won *what*?" The anger was gone from Alex's voice, replaced by confusion.

But Nick wasn't going to be drawn in. "The game. The prize. The *money*."

"Walk me through it." Alex stepped closer, peering at Nick as if he genuinely wanted to understand. "Was this the plan from the start? Was... you and me. All that stuff. Was that part of your *game*?"

"No." Damn it. Nick wished he had a different answer. This whole thing would be easier if he *had* been manipulating Alex all along. But he had to tell the truth. "You and me was separate. It wasn't supposed to happen." He grinned quickly. "Like I said, old habits are hard to break."

"Just a habit," Alex echoed softly. Then he seemed to pull himself back to the conversation and said, "What about the rest of it? All planned?"

"I planned to get control of the company, sell off the most valuable assets, and sell my shares for a huge profit. The land..." What *had* that been about? "I was genuinely interested in buying it, at first. I knew about the heritage fight, but there're ways around that. I would have gone through with the purchase, at the price I first bid. But when Blake overbid me..." He shrugged as if the shock of the moment had been nothing. The grudging respect for the old bastard's refusal to roll over, the stab of disappointment that Blake hadn't acknowledged Nick's victory, and, of course, the old resentment over a father who cared more about winning at business than about his own son. None of that should be shared, not with Alex. Not with anyone. "I figured if he wanted to play rough, I'd play rough. That's all."

"And Liam?" Alex sounded bitter. "Was he just another pawn? Did you send him out to lie to your father on purpose?"

"He showed up, huh? I wasn't sure he would." Nick decided that the visit was the final justification he needed for canceling the credit card Liam had access to. "All I did was let him see a little bad information. I didn't ask him to spread it around, and I sure as hell didn't ask Blake to listen to him. But, yeah, I thought it might happen. Liam was pissed and he's petty, and Blake really likes to win."

"You're both insane," Alex said. "His daughter is lying in a hospital bed, fighting for her life, and the two of you are…" He broke off, then said, "He's going to lose it all. He's got a wife and two little kids, and all of them are going to be broke if this margin call spirals out of control. Which it will, if you don't do something to stop it."

"Me?" Nick fought back a disbelieving laugh. "You want me to fix it?" This was the part that Alex needed to understand, so Nick leaned in a little and spoke fiercely. "You want me to give up? I *won*, fair and square, playing the game he wanted to play, and now you want me to pretend I lost?"

"No." Alex sounded frustrated. "Is that all it is? Just a game? If it is, then fine, you won. Congratulations. You beat him. But now you could start a new game. A better game, one that *doesn't* end up with your father and his family out on the street." Alex seemed to think he was on to something. "How would you do it? If you wanted to bail him out, what would you do?"

"I could just give him money, if I wanted to. No big strategy needed. Hell, I could probably just make a deposit with his broker and then cosign on his loan." There was no way on earth Nick *would* do any of that, but he certainly could if he wanted to.

"But that would humiliate him even more," Alex said flatly. "You want him to know he lost? Trust me, he knows. Isn't there a way to let him save a little face?"

"I'm supposed to care about him saving face? Really?"

"He let you down. When you were a kid. I know that. He wasn't a great father before your mother died, and afterward… he did his best, but he wasn't what you wanted. I was there; I know. He wasn't as strong as you needed him to be. But I really think he was as strong as he *could* be. He was torn up with guilt. My mother's told me stories; she thought he was maybe going to do the same thing your mom did." Alex was still trained not to use the word, Nick noted. "She was really worried about it. She sat him down and told him it wasn't his fault. Your mom had a mental illness, and he did everything he could to get her help, but it just wasn't enough. He still blamed himself. But you know what he told my mother, Nick?" Alex's eyes were shining. "He told her not to worry; he couldn't do that to you. He said you'd been through too much already, and he wasn't enough of a bastard to abandon you."

Nick had never heard that story before; he wondered why. But he wasn't sure it changed anything. "It's not about revenge for what he did, or didn't do, when I was a kid. Maybe taking over the company was about that, a little. But the land deal? *He* started that, not me. He's a pathetic old man who couldn't accept that he'd lost, so he gambled too much and lost even bigger."

"'A pathetic old man.' If that's all he is, take pity on him. Show a little compassion. You helped his daughter because she needed it and you could do it. Now he needs help, and you could give it to him."

Alex's eyes were pleading, and it was hard to look away. Damn it. Blake hadn't been there for Nick growing up, but Alex always had. And now he was asking for a favor. If it had been anything else, saying yes would have been easy. Even after all the years apart, Alex could have anything that was in Nick's power to give. But why did it have to be this?

"You could be the bigger man," Alex said softly. "*That* could be your victory. Maybe Blake wouldn't understand it, but that would be his loss. You'd know. And I'd know. You won the game, and then you stepped up and won something even bigger."

Nick couldn't keep up with this. "Damn, you're wasting your talents in corporate law. Not many opportunities for big impassioned speeches at work, huh? You saved it all up for me. I'm flattered."

But Alex apparently hadn't lost his ability to shrug off Nick's smart-ass comments. "There isn't much time." He moved as if he were going to reach out to Nick, but caught himself and returned his hands to his sides. "Help him, Nick. Please. Maybe he doesn't deserve it, but you can do it anyway."

Nick had no idea what to say. This was *not* part of the plan. He shuffled out of Alex's way and watched him walk to the doorway. Alex opened the door and looked back as if about to give a few parting words, but instead he shrugged and smiled. Then he stepped out into the hallway, closed the door behind him, and was gone.

Nick sank into a chair, leaned forward with his elbows on his knees, and held his head between his hands. He squeezed, trying to fit the conflicting thoughts together somehow. His mother. Blake. Winning. Alex.

"Fuck," he growled, and then pulled out his phone and found the number he needed. When his broker answered, he said, "It's Nick Colton. You're going to think I'm insane, but I want you to buy back the SeaCo shares I just sold. The price is still falling, right?" He listened to his broker's confused confirmation. "So I'll still make a profit. I sold high; I'm buying low, at least at the start. It's not the stupidest thing I've ever done. Not quite."

He dealt with the technicalities and his broker's cautious protestations, and then he hung up the phone. He was tempted to throw it against the wall. He never could win in Seattle; that was apparently some sort of cosmic rule. He shouldn't have come back to town, and he should have stayed away from Alex. He absolutely never should have let himself fall back in… Wait. He'd fallen into *bed* with Alex. That was all. And then he'd been swayed by loyalty to an old friend. It was a weakness, but it wasn't terrible. Now he could get the hell out of Seattle and never think about any of it again. A couple of days to wrap things up, and he'd be gone. Rosa had been crazy, and he'd been stupid to listen to her. Whatever he and Alex used to have, it was long gone. If Alex had still cared, he wouldn't have been so quick to take Blake's side. He would have celebrated Nick's victory instead of insisting that it become a surrender. Alex didn't care about Nick, and Nick had to make himself not care about Alex. He just had to… what? He was back to feeling helpless. Nick stared at the suite's mini-bar for a moment, then walked purposely toward it. He needed to forget. Or remember, maybe. He needed to remember all the pain, all the resentment and anger of his last departure from Seattle.

He didn't want to wait for a bellhop to bring up ice, so he poured the little bottle of Chivas into a glass neat and took a long sip. Yeah, he needed to remember. He'd felt this way about Alex before, and it had almost destroyed him. He wouldn't go through that kind of pain again.

Alex had given up on them. Alex had chosen conventionality and safety over Nick. And he would do it again. Nick had to remember that.

He knocked back the rest of his drink and stared out at the once-familiar skyline. Alex didn't love him. That was the important thing to remember. He looked down at the empty glass in his hand and headed back to the fridge to see what else looked good.

CHAPTER EIGHTEEN

Nick had come through. Alex still wasn't sure he believed it. It hadn't been Alex's words, he was sure; Nick hadn't seemed too impressed by those. It had been Nick's innate goodness, his compassion. As hard as he tried to cover it up, it always ended up shining through.

It took Blake a while to understand what was happening. When Alex returned to the house, the first margin call had just gone through. Twenty percent of Blake's shares had been sold, but for some reason, the stock price wasn't falling. Blake and Alex and Helena sat in the office staring at the computer screen, watching as the stock price stayed steady, and then started to rise.

"What's happening?" Blake muttered in disbelief.

Alex didn't say anything, even when Blake turned to him and demanded, "What the hell did you do?"

"Don't ask too many questions," Helena said, her hand gripping Blake's tightly. "Just hope it keeps working."

It did. Alex wasn't sure how much money Nick was sinking into the company, but it was enough to keep the share price high. Enough to let Blake keep the rest of his shares, at least temporarily. He was still badly overextended as a result of his stupidity, but he hadn't lost everything.

It was Helena who figured it out. She shifted her focus from the computer to Alex and softly said, "Nick?"

Blake stared at her in confusion. "Nick? What about him?"

"He's the one buying the shares. Right, Alex?"

Alex nodded. "I think so. I don't know for sure. Maybe it's somebody else, taking a chance on some undervalued stock. But... yeah. I think it's Nick."

"Why?" Blake sounded genuinely mystified. "What's he up to

now?"

"He's a good person," Helena said softly. "He's helping his family."

"He's the one who got his family into this mess in the first place!"

"No, Blake." Helena gave her husband a loving smile but shook her head firmly. "He's not. He started it, maybe. But you're the one who couldn't let go. You're the one who came up with the bidding nonsense."

"So I should have just walked away? Let him get away with it?"

"Would that have been so bad?" Alex had no idea why he was getting involved in this, but he didn't seem to be able to stop himself. "To have let Nick win? I mean, he did anyway, after all was said and done."

"Nick won, and I lost." Blake stared at Alex. "That's what you think?"

"What I think? Yeah, if that's how you want to put it. It just seems like reality."

"So you've chosen his side." Blake's voice was almost threatening.

"His side? I'm the one who got him to start buying shares back, Blake. So you—and your family—don't lose everything." Alex was still wound up from seeing Nick, and Blake's accusation sent another surge of adrenaline through his body. He needed to get out of there before he said something he'd regret. He knew what he *wanted* to say. *Yeah, I guess I have chosen a side. It's way the hell over here, away from whatever you and Nick are doing to each other.* God, it would feel good. He could say, *Nick's smart and he knows what he's doing. If you're stupid enough to fuck with him again, I won't do a damned thing about it.* The words burbled around in his throat, and he almost choked as he forced himself to swallow them. "I should go," he managed. Blake didn't answer, so Alex turned and left.

He didn't realize Helena was following him until he heard her say his name just as he was pulling open the front door. "Alex!" she called, coming closer and pressing his hand between hers. "Thank you. For helping him. For helping all of us."

"It was Nick, not me," Alex said. "You said it before: he's a good person. All I did was remind him of that."

She smiled. "Well, thank you for that. And I'm sorry Blake was rude. He's... he's having a hard time with all of this. He's always been so proud. It's hard for him to be beaten." She raised her eyebrows. "But that doesn't make it all right for him to be a jackass. He's just giving himself one more thing to be embarrassed about."

"He needs to be careful. Loyalty tests, wounded pride... things didn't turn out too well for King Lear."

"I don't think I'll bring that reference to his attention," Helena said. "But I will try to get him back on an even keel. I'm sure he'll call you in a few days."

"I'm not sure I'll answer," Alex said. "I'm pretty tired of all this. I think I'd like to stay away from the Colton soap opera for a little while."

Helena nodded. "I can understand that. But, Alex, don't stay away from your mother, okay? She's been worried about you; she says you aren't talking to her. I don't know what's going on between you and Nick, but Blake and Rosa both seem to think there's something. Whatever it is..." Helena shrugged. "Talk to your mother. She's worried."

Of course. His mom had been the one who best understood how much he had loved Nick. She'd been the one who'd seen his pain after Nick left. Alex had worked to shield her from it, but he knew some had slipped through. Now she'd be worried that he was going to fall back under Nick's spell. "I'll give her a call," he promised, but he didn't say when. "Take care of yourself, Helena."

"Thank you, Alex." There was a strange extra intensity to her voice as she added, "You take care of yourself, too."

He drove back downtown trying not to think about anything related to anyone named Colton. He turned the radio up loud and found songs he could sing along to. He wondered how much he'd let slip at work while he'd been distracted by the SeaCo nonsense. He reminded himself to pick up his dry cleaning and buy some groceries. And then he found himself parked not in his own building's garage, but down the street from Nick's hotel.

Nick didn't seem surprised to see Alex on his doorstep for the second time that day. He just stepped back and let Alex come inside. Once the door was closed behind him, Alex stopped in front of Nick, too shy to look him in the eyes, and lifted one tentative hand, fingers curled until their backs brushed the buttons of Nick's shirt.

Nick's strong hand caught Alex's wrist and pushed him back roughly. "No," he snarled, stalking into the room to stand looking out the window.

Alex felt cold. What had happened? What had he done? He followed Nick into the room and stood there, waiting like a schoolboy in the principal's office. But Nick didn't say anything, so finally Alex asked, "What's wrong?"

"I did what you wanted, Alex. But I'm done playing your games." He reached for the glass on the windowsill, and Alex knew the amber liquid in it wasn't tea this time.

"I'm not—I came over to thank you…"

"And to give me my reward for jumping through your hoop?" Nick turned and looked Alex up and down. "You didn't bother to put a bow on yourself? Or is it hidden under your clothes?"

Alex's head was whirling. "No." He struggled to think what he wanted to say. "I just… I don't know. I didn't plan this. I just wanted to thank you."

"Fine. You're welcome. Now get out." Nick drained his glass and yanked open the minibar, pulling a handful of little bottles out and twisting one open without looking at the label.

"Is this why you stopped drinking? Because you're a mean drunk?"

"I'm an *honest* drunk. And yeah, that's why I stopped. Honesty is *not* usually the best policy." Nick poured the liquor—clear,

Poor Little Rich Boy   153

so probably vodka or rum—into his glass before turning to Alex. "But I guess I don't have to remind you of that. I should probably be bowing down and genuflecting in front of the God of Lying, really."

"I don't understand why you're so angry, Nick. What did I do?"

"Not a damned thing." Nick pulled a sip of liquor through his teeth, then set the glass on the sideboard in apparent disgust. "You never do. Mister Perfect doesn't step a foot out of line—that's why you're in such a great position to judge me, right? Poor, stupid Nick, can't do the right thing unless we tell him what it is." Nick turned back toward the window. "I'm lucky to have you and my father, Alex. Really. The two of you are a perfect fucking team."

It was hard to sort the issues from the anger, but Alex tried. "I'm sorry if you felt I was judging you. I wasn't. You and your father—I don't understand that. I don't even try. But I sure as hell don't blame you for what's gone wrong in the relationship. I just walked out of your father's house to avoid having a fight with him about how stupid he's been."

Nick looked up, and for a beautiful moment Alex thought his smile was genuine. But then it twisted just a little. "And that would have been a tragedy, if the two of you fought. How could you possibly survive without his approval?"

"That's what you're angry about?" Alex felt his own temper rising. "The fact that I care about other people? That I try to take responsibility for the way my actions affect those people?"

Nick stared at him and the anger slowly faded from his face, leaving him looking sad, maybe even hurt. "You're right," he said quietly. "You take care of the people you really care about. They're lucky to have you."

Alex needed time to think this through. Things were going unsaid, and he was pretty sure Nick was interpreting the conversation very differently than Alex had intended. But Nick didn't seem inclined to give him that time. "So, thanks for coming by," Nick said, nodding toward the door. "I'm sure you and Blake will be back to normal in no time."

"I didn't mean I didn't care about you," Alex said. He knew it was too late, and he wasn't saying it right, but he tried anyway. "Before. When I... you know. When we were kids. It wasn't because I didn't care about you."

Nick nodded. "Okay."

"No, I mean it. I cared. A lot."

"Not enough, I guess." Nick found his glass and took another drink, then gave a quick, sad smile. "Obviously."

"No, Nick..." Alex stepped forward, but the look on Nick's face kept him from getting too close. "I cared more about you than about anyone else. Ever."

"Don't be stupid, Alex. Your mom told you to dump me, so you did. I know Rosa; there were no threats that you'd lose your family if you didn't cut me loose, nothing like that. She just said you should, so you did. She had her opinion of what was best, and you couldn't possibly disagree with that. You didn't believe in *us* enough to stand up to her." Another drink, and it was like he could sense Alex's blood in the water. "Was my father in on it, too? He always knew you could do better. I'm sure he *loves* your fiancée, right?" Nick's smile was fierce, now, and full of sharp teeth. "Maybe you cared about me, sort of. But not nearly enough. Jesus, Alex, I would have set myself on fire for you."

"I was weak," Alex said slowly. It hurt to admit it, but it was true. He and Nick had grown around each other like two young trees with their trunks entwined, and they'd been perfect together. But Alex hadn't been strong enough to fight for their love.

"Well, you're better now," Nick said with forced, sarcastic bonhomie. "Corporate law, engaged to a woman, tidying up after my father... you've come a long way. You're living your own life, now, for sure."

"You think it's easy for me?" Alex hissed. "Did you ever think that maybe the reason I had to work so hard to please them was because I was picking up your slack? Maybe if you'd done a little, I wouldn't have to have worked so hard."

"And you made damn sure I did my penance for that, Alex. I just poured almost seventy million dollars back into a company I no longer have any interest in, because you said I should. I gave the marrow of my fucking bones to a little girl because..." He stopped. "No. That wasn't penance. I did that because I was the only one who could." It seemed important to him that he not include the donation in his list of grievances. And catching himself seemed to have drained the energy right out of him. He shook his head. "I'm done, Alex. Go back to your lies. I hope they make everyone you care about very, very happy."

There was something to say. Some words that would make all this better. But Alex couldn't think of what they were, and Nick had the door to the suite open, waiting for him to leave. He walked slowly forward, obedient to the end, but when he was in the hallway he stopped and turned around. His mind was racing, searching for a way to fix this. Not for himself, to soothe his own hurts, but for Nick, because it wasn't fair that he should feel betrayed and alone after all he had done. But Nick didn't even look at him. He just shut the door in Alex's face.

It was over.

CHAPTER NINETEEN

Nick set his bag by the front door of the suite and walked back in to give the place a final once-over. He traveled pretty light and he hadn't brought anything that would be irreplaceable if he left it behind, but he had a hotel-leaving routine and he liked to follow it. He was developing a bit of a Seattle-leaving routine too, he mused. Alienate everyone, fight with Alex, get the fuck out of town. This time he'd had to stick around for a few days first and tidy things up with SeaCo. He wanted to make sure the place was going to be properly managed until the market was strong enough for him to start selling again. The relationship stuff, though; that was better left alone.

There was a knock at the door and he went to answer it. He pulled the door open and stopped short. "You're not the bellhop," he managed.

"No." Alex lifted his hands to show Nick an iPad. The image on the screen was moving, and as Nick tried to figure out what was going on, he saw a small blonde head appear.

"Nick!" Adrianna said excitedly, peering at what was obviously another screen at her end. "Hi!"

"Hi." He looked at Alex for an explanation, but Alex just jerked the tablet a little, making it clear that Nick should take it. Nick refused to give a damn about hurting Alex's feelings, but he didn't want to be rude to the little girl. So he took the tablet and angled it so the small picture of him in the corner of the screen seemed more-or-less focused on his face. "Are you feeling better?" he asked.

"I'm super-charged!" she practically yelled. "No joke. I'm still supposed to be careful about germs, and I still have to take some pills, but no more chemo! And I got…" she looked at someone behind the camera as she carefully said "en-graft-ment. That means it's working! The new cells are moving in and having babies."

"That's really good news, Adrianna. I'm really happy to hear that." He didn't have to force his smile anymore. Something good had come out of this trip after all. Something *very* good. "What's the next step?"

"I have to stay here a while longer. Because of germs. But I get to go home for the barbecue! And maybe even stay overnight."

"Nice. When's that?"

"Two weeks." Adrianna's expression got a little more serious. "Mommy said you might not be here for that. She said you had to go home. Are you going home?"

"Yeah, I am." Nick had no idea why he added, "But I like talking to you like this. Maybe we could do this again sometime, but from further away. I'd be way over in New York, and you'd be in Seattle."

"And you could come visit again," Adrianna said confidently.

"Well, maybe you could come see me. Have you ever been to New York?"

Another look to whoever was off-screen, and then a tentative nod. "Yes?"

Helena's voice prompted, "When you were little."

Adrianna looked at Nick and solemnly said, "When I was very little."

"Well, if you're out there again, you should let me know. Or, you know... your mom could give me a call." That wouldn't be a nightmare, probably. When Helena wasn't in rabid-mother mode, she seemed fairly civilized.

"Mommy says we can get a puppy, but not yet. Not until I'm more better."

"Nice. You should get a big one." What kind of dog would leave the most impact on Blake's orderly, sanitized life? "Maybe a Newfoundland, or a Saint Bernard." Something with a lot of hair, and hopefully a similar amount of drool.

"Probably something smaller," Helena's voice said, and Adrianna made a face.

Then she picked a piece of paper up from the table beside her and pushed it in front of the camera. "I made this picture for you," she said. "See? That's me, and you, and that's Mommy and Daddy, and that's Damon. See you and me? We both have purple in us."

"Yeah… what's that about?"

"It's the super-charge," Adrianna said as if it should be obvious, and Nick had to admit it made sense now that it had been explained.

"That's a great picture, Adrianna." A total fantasy, of course; all the people in the picture had big smiles and seemed happy to be standing next to each other. "Maybe you should add that dog in, so nobody forgets about it."

"Okay. And then I'll send it to you. Mommy says we have your address. Okay?"

"Absolutely. I look forward to getting it."

"Okay, Anna," came Helena's voice. "Say bye for now."

"Bye for now," Adrianna said obediently, then leaned forward and pressed a kiss against the screen.

"Bye, Adrianna," Nick said.

He was about to hand the tablet back to Alex when Helena's face appeared. The image was bouncing a little, and Nick realized that she was walking. A few moments later it stilled and she said, "She wants to stay in touch with you, Nick. It's important to her."

It wasn't as terrible a thought as he'd have imagined. "Yeah. Okay. You have my contact information. I'll start sending Christmas presents; maybe you can email me suggestions or something."

"It's not about gifts. You already gave her the most important present anyone ever could. And I know you're busy. But… please. If you can. Let her in your life, just a little bit."

Surprisingly, it didn't feel like a trap. "Okay. But I don't know anything about kids, Helena. You'll have to give me tips."

"What's that, Nick? You want me to tell you what to do?" Her smile was mischievous. "Well, if you insist…"

"Within reason," he added quickly with a smile of his own. "Take care of her, okay? She's a good kid."

"Next time we talk, I'm going to nag you about getting to know Damon. He's a good kid, too, and he'd really like a brother." And now the trapped feeling was coming. Helena seemed to sense it even through the camera and raised her hands quickly. "Okay, okay. Not the *next* time. But eventually. Brace yourself."

"I've been warned," Nick agreed. "Thanks for setting this up, Helena."

"Thank Alex. It was his idea." She smiled again, then reached an arm forward. The screen turned black.

Nick took a deep breath. "Thanks," he said, extending the tablet in Alex's direction. But Alex didn't take it.

Instead, he stepped forward, still just barely inside the hotel room, and said, "Can I show you a few more things? I've been busy. Since... you know. Since we last talked."

"I was out of line, Alex. It's not my place to judge your life."

"No, it's not. But you were right." He paused, still waiting for Nick's permission. "Can I come in?"

Nick's clean getaway was looking less and less likely, but he couldn't refuse Alex. He stepped backward and Alex edged inside and let the door close behind him. Then he eased over beside Nick and hit a couple icons on the screen. A PDF of a business letter appeared and Alex looked up expectantly.

Nick turned the screen sideways and read the first few words. Then he turned to Alex. "Jesus. Did you send this?"

"Two days ago."

"You quit your job. The big downtown firm... you quit."

"I don't want to practice corporate law, Nick. I honestly can't even remember why I applied there in the first place. I just did it. But it's not what I want."

"Damn. That's..." What the hell was it? What sort of reaction was Alex looking for, here? "Congratulations. Do you know what you want to do instead?"

"I've made a few calls. I'm thinking I'd really like to get into public-interest law."

"Just like you always said."

"Yeah." Alex looked at Nick as if gauging his reaction, then leaned over and hit the screen a few more times. This time he pulled up an e-mail, and again Nick obediently read the first few words before looking up and shaking his head.

"No, Alex—I shouldn't be reading this."

"Yeah, you should. It's addressed to her, but it's telling her about *my* thoughts and feelings, and I want you to know those. I want you to understand."

"No." Nick tried to return the tablet. Alex wouldn't take it from him, but he couldn't force Nick to look at it.

After they stared at each other long enough to establish a stalemate, Alex sighed. "Okay, then I'll tell you what it says. I told her I couldn't go through with the engagement. I told her I was trying to respect her decision not to talk to me about it, but I needed to make it clear to both of us that we aren't engaged anymore. I still care about her, and respect her, and I really, really want to do whatever I can to help her be okay. But I'm gay, and I want to live my life as who I am, not as who other people want me to be. That's what I told her."

Nick was afraid he might be gaping like a fish. "Jesus, you don't do things halfway, do you? Are you okay? You're making a lot of changes really fast."

"But wait, there's more." Another few taps on the screen, and Alex was looking at a picture of a vaguely familiar door. It was the Díaz's back door, the one that led into their kitchen, he realized. The glass in the doorframe was broken in a long, jagged line.

"What happened? Is everyone okay?"

Alex nodded. "They will be." He moved so he could look Nick in the eyes. "My dad slammed the door so hard it broke the glass. That was after I told him and my mom that I'm gay. After I told them that Marta and I wouldn't be getting married." Alex took a deep breath and his expression was pleading. Desperate. "After I told them that I'm in love with Nick Colton. That I always had been and always will be."

Nick was frozen. Not just his body, but his brain. It stuttered into motion, replayed the phrase "in love with Nick Colton," and froze up again.

"I did it for *me*," Alex said quickly. "I'm not trying to pressure you into anything. I did it *because* of you, because you made me want to be better. I wanted to tell the truth, and the truth is, I never got over you. And if all these years haven't done it, then..."

Nick's brain still didn't work, but apparently his body was able to operate independently. That was the only explanation for the warm skin and gently curling hair he could suddenly feel beneath his fingertips. And for the hard line of Alex's body being pulled forward, the delicious strength molding itself to conform to the demands of Nick's arms. Nick may not have given the order to move, but he was making no complaints as his lips found Alex's in a hungry kiss.

When Nick's brain finally returned to action, it was in a primal mode. He wanted to control, claim, and possess, and Alex seemed fine with being the object of all that. He let Nick back him up against the wall, then pull his arms up over his head. One of Nick's hands stayed up there, holding Alex's arms out of the way, and his other hand explored. He jerked fabric out of the way impatiently, running his fingers along Alex's warm ribcage. He could feel each shallow, excited breath, the quick gasps and trembling exhalations between kisses. He tweaked a nipple, then slid his hand down over Alex's abs, around to his back, and down until he ran into the waistband of Alex's chinos.

"Too many clothes," he said firmly.

"So do something about it."

Nick was ready to do a *lot* about it, but then there was another knock at the door. They both froze, and Nick felt the first flash of doubt. Was this real? Alex had said the words, but did he really understand what they meant?

He pushed away a little, and the knock came again. "Mr.

Colton? I'm here for your bags."

Nick looked at Alex, leaning against the wall, doubts starting to show on his face as well. "You're leaving," Alex said. "You have to go. I sprang this on you, and you haven't had time to think about it, and I wasn't looking for anything to happen. I mean, it would be great if it did, but like I said, I wanted to tell you for *me*, because I wanted to be honest for a change, and…"

Alex stopped babbling when Nick ran a gentle finger over his lips.

Alex had taken a chance. He'd found the strength to expose himself to the people he cared about, and Nick was one of the people on that list. "I changed my mind," he said, loudly enough that the bellhop could hear through the doorway. "Tell the desk I'm not checking out today."

There was a pause, then, "Should I tell them how much longer you plan to stay?"

Nick looked at Alex and let his body sag in a little, not to press, just to brush together. "Tell them I'm staying indefinitely," he said firmly. In a quieter voice just for Alex he said, "Forever. Tell them I'm staying forever."

CHAPTER TWENTY

Alex still had one sock on. The rest of his clothes had been peeled off by Nick's practiced hands, but somehow that one sock had been missed. Alex could have done something about it himself, but his body was no longer under his control. Every nerve ending, every muscle fiber, every drop of blood in his veins: they were all obedient to Nick.

"You're beautiful," Nick murmured as he kissed the hollow above Alex's collarbone. "Perfect."

There was no breath in Alex's lungs for objections, so he just accepted the statement. He was with Nick, after all, and they were perfect together, so it made sense. "I love you," he said, so softly he wasn't sure Nick would hear. But Nick's mouth flattened against Alex's skin and sucked almost painfully in response to the words. Alex arched up into the sensation and let his mind and body float into the sea of pleasure.

When Nick was finally satisfied, he licked the mark he'd left and smiled in catlike satisfaction. "You're mine."

"I'll get a tattoo, if you want." Alex said it lightly, but he was deadly serious. He'd do whatever Nick wanted, whatever it took. He ran his hand over his upper chest and said, "'Property of Nick Colton.'"

Nick's eyes lit up when Alex said that, a hungry fire Alex hadn't seen before. As boys, they'd been so confident of their mutual desires that there had been no need for declarations or symbols. But now, apparently, things were different. Nick shifted over so his body was hovering over Alex's, their cocks brushing tantalizingly along Alex's stomach, their nipples aligned. "Really only me?" Nick asked.

Alex nodded as soon as he understood what Nick was asking. "The only man. Ever."

"We need to go slow," Nick said reluctantly. "You know…"

"I want you inside me," Alex interrupted. "I mean, if you want to. I want to."

That earned Alex a deep kiss, and Nick's hips began moving slowly as he lowered himself, letting Alex take more of his weight and letting their cocks rub in a maddening, rhythmic dance. "I don't want to hurt you."

"We did it before. I liked it." Alex concentrated on kissing back, and reached around to find Nick's ass and pull him down for closer contact. "I want to do it again." Alex wanted to do *everything*, really, but especially this. The new dynamic, the claiming and marking… Alex would have gone along with it just to help satisfy Nick, but he was finding that he wanted it, too. He'd been alone for too long and he wanted to be claimed, even if it was only for a little while. He wanted to belong to Nick in every possible way. "I want you to fuck me."

"Jesus, Alex," Nick groaned, and then his mouth was on Alex's neck again, sucking and marking. Alex gasped in appreciation and tilted his head away to give Nick more room. He wanted this as much as Nick did. Maybe their mutual need for identifying marks was a problematic sign of insecurity, but Alex really didn't care. It felt perfect.

When Nick was satisfied, at least temporarily, he pulled his face away from Alex's neck and looked up at him. The same blue eyes that had gazed at Alex with so much trust and affection years ago, looking up at him now with a hint of doubt. "You're sure about this?"

"Do I need to show you the evidence again? The extensive digital documentation?" And just because he could, Alex guided Nick's hand down to their hard, leaking cocks. "And Exhibit B, if you need more reassurance."

"I don't mean the gay part." Nick's grin was quick, and so familiar it sent a quiver of pleasure and pain through Alex's chest. "I could have told you that a long time ago. As I think I've already reminded you, I *did* tell you that a long time ago."

"And then you helped me test the theory."

For a moment, Alex thought the words were going to send

Nick's mouth to find another spot to mark, but instead, his expression turned serious. "You know, when I left... I left because I didn't want you to get hurt. But I stayed away because *I* didn't want to get hurt. I didn't want to be here and have to watch you move on with your life. I didn't anticipate the 'dating women' thing, I admit. I figured you'd end up with some other guy. And I didn't want to see that."

"I'm sorry," Alex started, but Nick shook his head.

"That's not what I mean. I just... don't you think you should be with other guys, at least for a while? You've only ever been with me. So all this stuff you think you're feeling for me... how can you know if it's really about me, or just about the fact that I have the right equipment?" Alex didn't know where this was coming from. How did they go from where they were five minutes—hell, *two* minutes ago, to this? Or... was Nick getting cold feet? Things had happened pretty fast; Nick had planned to be on an airplane right now, headed back to the life he'd built for himself, not here in bed with Alex. It had seemed too good to be true; maybe it was. Maybe Alex needed to start bracing himself for a goodbye after all.

Nick shifted away, frowning. He eased back onto his knees, and wrapped the sheet around his hips as if shielding himself. "So," he said quietly. "The thing is, I still can't do it. Everything you said about how after all these years you still felt the same, that's true for me, too. But I *have* been out there, meeting other guys, fucking around, so I know." He shook his head. "None of those guys came anywhere *close* to what you mean to me. I said I'd stay, but I can't sit here and watch that.. You need to—"

"Stop. Rewind," Alex managed to say.

Nick looked at him in puzzlement. "What? What do you mean?"

"Go back to the part where you said it was true for you, too. The part where you said you hadn't found anything like you and me." Alex's whole body was tense, wanting to believe but waiting for the 'but...' that would carry Nick out of the room and back out of Alex's life again.

Nick shook his head. "What? Jesus, Alex, do you think I stayed away all this time because I didn't like the fucking *climate*? I thought I was strong enough to come back and not fall for you again, but that was stupid, 'cause I was never out of love with you in the first place."

Alex's breath caught. "Repeat," he whispered.

"Repeat? Repeat what?"

"The part about love." Alex knew his eyes were wide, staring at Nick's face as if it held all the secrets of the universe.

"No." Nick shifted a bit further away. "I was doing okay, Alex, and I need to keep it that way. I can't—"

"You love me," Alex said softly. "You just said it. You said you were never out of love with me. That means you love me now."

Nick's face twisted into an almost tortured expression. "Yeah. It does. But..."

Alex didn't think he'd ever moved so fast. He shifted around, drove up onto his knees and grabbed hold of Nick's head. Now it was his turn to pull a shocked body toward his own, his turn to push into a kiss, and finally, his turn to feel the initial resistance fade into stunned compliance. When Nick relaxed, Alex pulled his mouth away just far enough that he could murmur, "I love you. I don't want other men, I want *you*. Always. Only you."

"But..." Nick began, but he subsided and let Alex kiss him into silence. Alex pulled the sheet loose from Nick's hips so they were naked against each other again, the way they should always be.

"I won't hurt you, Nick. Never again. I'm so sorry I did it the first time. Sorry for you, and sorry for me, too."

Alex could actually see the moment when Nick let himself believe. Nick's whole face relaxed. He stopped looking like a millionaire businessman with the weight of the world on his shoulders, and transformed into the boy Alex had known, golden and smiling, blue eyes gazing at Alex with absolute faith and love. "Okay," Nick whispered.

"Okay," Alex agreed. He wrapped his hand around Nick's cock and said, "Now, I think we had a plan for this."

Nick grinned quickly. "Yeah. But it doesn't have to be now, Alex. It's been a long time. You're probably…"

"Really fucking horny," Alex finished. "I want your hands on me, and I want your mouth, but right now, I want you inside me." He leaned back a little. "You going to turn me down?"

Another shy grin, and then Nick moved sideways, shifting off the bed and tugging Alex to join him. "C'mon," he said.

Alex thought about resisting, or at least asking questions, but he didn't. He stepped off the bed and waited for instructions. Nick took his hand and led him toward the bathroom, which was just as modern and luxurious as the rest of the suite. They stopped beside the large, glassed-in shower stall and Nick said, "Turn the water on and get in. I'll be right back." He stopped after a single step and said, "You're going to take that sock off, right?"

Alex bent and removed it with a flourish, and Nick grinned at him before disappearing.

With Nick's words of doubt still ringing in his head, Alex was frightened to let him go, even as far as the next room. He was tempted to follow Nick just to make sure he didn't make a break for it, but forced himself to turn the water on and get into the shower instead.

To Alex's relief, Nick returned almost immediately. Alex's eyes, after their initial appreciation of the long lines of the naked body in front of him, were drawn to the tube and the square foil packets Nick had retrieved—but apparently Alex looked a little too long, because Nick started backpedaling again. "Still totally optional," he said. "Or, you know… I don't usually, but we can switch it around, if you want…"

"What I want is for you to quit freaking out and fuck me," Alex said.

Nick stepped into the shower, set the supplies on the wooden bench, and ran his hands almost tentatively over Alex's shoulders and down to his waist. "If it's just because you think it's what I expect, think again. Lots of couples never do. There's other ways to get off."

Alex let himself savor the word *couple* for a moment, but then shook his head. "For fuck's sake, Nick, I'm not a virgin. We've done this before. I know it's been a long time, but I haven't forgotten how much I liked it. And as I recall, you seemed to like it, too."

Now it was Nick's shoulders that relaxed. Damn. It had started with his face, and now reached his torso... Alex had better shut up before the relaxing trend hit his cock. Alex leaned forward and Nick kissed him—softly at first, then with increasing heat—under the shower's warm spray.

Alex really couldn't let himself think about how Nick had gotten so good at this. Nick's hands were confident as they ran over Alex's body, massaging him with a shower gel Alex hadn't even noticed him opening. Chest and arms first, then firm strokes up and down Alex's aching cock, and then back over his ass before sliding gently between his cheeks.

Alex let himself relax into Nick's ministrations, arching his back to present his ass for more attention, and Nick seemed happy to comply. His fingers kneaded Alex's flesh, delved toward his opening, then eased away. He kissed a path down Alex's spine, his hands traveling further down to massage Alex's thighs and calves before returning to the crucial spot, running his thumbs down the crease, and then, Jesus Christ, something soft and warm that could only be Nick's tongue. They had never done *that* before, and Alex could feel his muscles tighten in surprise.

Nick obviously felt it, too. He stood, wrapped his arms around Alex's chest, and rested his chin on his shoulder. "You don't like that?"

"I have no idea! I mean... I've heard about it. But I don't... I have no idea. You're okay with it?"

"I think you're clean enough right now." Nick kissed Alex's neck. "It's a good way to relax you, but obviously that won't work if you don't like it. Your call."

"I trust you," Alex said. "If you think I'll like it, and you don't mind doing it... let's give it a try."

"Just tell me if you want me to stop," Nick said firmly, and Alex turned his head to capture Nick's mouth in an awkward, perfect kiss.

This time when Nick's fingers returned, Alex knew what they were preparing for, and he made himself relax. Warmth, gentle suction, a lapping tongue, soft kisses... Alex let his mind turn off, and his body sagged and arched in pleasure. When Nick's fingers came back into play, pressing and stretching, exploring and withdrawing, it felt as if every drop of energy and awareness in Alex's body rushed outwards, searching for contact with Nick.

Alex was so lost in pleasure he barely noticed that Nick had straightened up until he felt a gentle brush of stubble against his cheek. "Ready?" Nick murmured.

Alex could only moan in reply, but apparently the wanton, welcoming tilt of his hips sent the right message. Nick kissed his neck, and then there was blunt pressure, and a stretch, and then Nick was inside him, sliding as easily as coming home.

Alex didn't even try to remain conscious of the details. There would be other times with Nick, other chances to catalogue and study and understand. This time was just for the sensations. Pressure, gentle friction, rough kisses and nips soothed by a warm tongue, Nick's hands teasing and claiming. As his climax built, Alex became aware of other sensations, more emotional than physical. Nick's body was behind him, warm and strong; Nick's arms were wrapped around him and cushioning him from the hard tile wall; Nick's voice was murmuring encouragement and reassurances. Alex felt safe. He felt loved. He felt Nick, and that was all he had ever needed.

EPILOGUE

The house looked the same, but it didn't look like home anymore. Which made sense, of course. It had been more than ten years since Nick had lived there, and even then it had been more of a residence than a real home. Still, he'd expected something more, some emotional reaction that just wasn't happening. He turned to Alex and shrugged. "Okay. Let's get it over with."

"What a fantastic attitude for a family gathering." Alex's words might be sarcastic, but his tone was warm and his fingers laced through Nick's with a squeeze of understanding.

"Hey, guys!" The female voice came from behind them, and they turned to see Jani coming up the broad stone walkway carrying a covered casserole dish. "You bracing yourselves?" She got a little closer. "'Cause you should be. I talked to Mami last night, and she still wasn't sure if Papi was going to come."

"Jesus," Alex groaned, and Nick frowned at Jani. She was on their side; their first outing as a couple had been dinner at her place, and in the weeks since then she'd been reliably warm and supportive. But she seemed to take an inordinate amount of joy in seeing Alex squirm.

"Little sisters," Nick said reprovingly. "They don't *have* to be bratty, I don't think. Adrianna doesn't seem to enjoy seeing me suffer."

"You're still a novelty. Give her time." Jani stretched up and kissed each of them on the cheek. "And give Papi time, too. Even if he doesn't show up today, he'll come around eventually."

"Might actually be better *not* to have the big reunion scene in public," Nick said, hoping to find a bright side. "Maybe you guys could go for a beer sometime, and…"

"Too late," Alex said quietly. Nick and Jani turned to follow his gaze and saw Rosa and Andrés walking up from the parking area.

Nick tried to let go of Alex's hand and was surprised by the strength with which his fingers were squeezed. "No," Alex said firmly. "I've wasted too much time already. I'm not going to start hiding again. I won't."

"You don't have to *flaunt* it, either," Nick suggested.

"Holding hands isn't flaunting," Alex replied. "If I'd do it on a public street, I can damn well do it in front of my father."

Jani raised her eyebrows. "My brother, the gay-rights activist."

"Your brother, the family member," Alex shot back. "Who should be accepted for who he is, not who they wish he were."

Jani smiled at Alex, then turned back to Nick and stretched up to give him another quick kiss. "Thank you," she said seriously, "for being the Prince Charming who woke up my sleeping brother."

Nick wasn't quite sure how to respond to that, and there wasn't time anyway, with Rosa and Andrés approaching.

"Hey, guys!" Jani said easily, stepping forward to greet her parents with kisses. Then she lifted the casserole dish. "This is getting heavy. I'm going to go set it down."

"I'll come with you," Rosa said quickly. She was carrying another casserole, and Nick was glad he and Alex had only been asked to bring buns and condiments. Grocery bags were easier to drop if Andrés decided to start swinging. "Good to see you, boys," Rosa said easily. She hadn't yet invited them to her home, but she'd been by Alex's place several times when Nick was there, and seemed friendly and easy with him.

No, the women of the family were not the concern. Nick wished he could escape with them and leave Alex to deal with his father alone, but that would be cowardly. Alex had a death grip on his fingers, anyway.

"We'll see you inside," Jani said, and she and her mother headed into the house.

There was an awkward pause. "It's good to see you again, Mr. Díaz," Nick tried.

Andrés stared at him for far too long before nodding jerkily. "Nick," he grunted. No *good to see you*, no *welcome back*. Under the circumstances, the absence of niceties wasn't too surprising, but it was pretty damned awkward.

"I'm glad you came, Papi," Alex said. "I know you're disappointed in me, but I'm glad you came."

Another long stare, and then Andrés shook his head vigorously. "No, Alejandro. I'm not disappointed in you. Not the way you mean. I'm…" he struggled for words. "I'm confused. About…" he waved his hand in Nick's general direction. "But I'm not disappointed because of what you're doing now. I'm… surprised? Hurt… and, yes, disappointed, by what you did for so long. Lying to us. Lying to Marta."

"Lying to myself," Alex said quietly. "I know that doesn't make it okay. But I honestly thought I could be who you wanted me to be. I did."

"You can," Andrés said firmly. "I want you to be *you*. And if that means you're…" another vague wave toward Nick, "then that's what it means. You're still my son." It seemed like the words were the culmination of a lot of thought, and Andrés spoke them as if he were tasting each syllable to be sure it was true.

Nick wasn't really enjoying his role as target of the hand-waving, but at least Alex seemed happy. "Thank you, Papi," he said, and he finally let go of Nick to give his father a hug. As he pulled away, he said quietly, "And the word's 'gay.' I'm gay, Papi."

Andrés looked at his son, then gave a quick jerk of his head as a nod. He didn't repeat the word, but at least Alex had said it. "Let's go inside," Andrés said, and stalked off, Nick and Alex trailing in his wake. This time, it was Nick who reached for Alex's hand, and the one who squeezed tight and wouldn't let go.

Helena greeted them at the doorway with kisses. Her face was bright, her eyes dancing, and they didn't really have to ask. But Nick did, anyway. "She's home, then? She's doing well?"

"We have to take her back tonight, but she's home for now." Helena nodded vigorously, then wrapped her arms around Nick and gave him a fierce hug. "Thank you," she whispered, and smiled at Alex over Nick's shoulder.

Nick was obviously uncomfortable with the appreciation, and he shrugged like a schoolboy. "So no big Greek curse, then? I've escaped?"

"For now," Helena agreed with a laugh. "But you'd better stay on my good side."

Alex stepped forward and raised the canvas grocery bags. "Buns, as ordered, and every kind of ketchup and mustard they had in the store. We're still okay, right?"

"I am pleased," Helena said regally, then hooked her arm through Andrés. "Let's go see what everyone's up to. We're set up out by the pool."

Nick and Alex trailed along behind. They were barely through the doorway when they heard a happy child's voice yelling, "Nick! Alex!"

Adrianna was beside them almost immediately, Damon trailing close behind. Nick crouched down, they threw their arms around his neck, and he stood easily, one arm supporting each child. "Hey, guys!" He kissed Damon on the temple, and Adrianna on the cheek just beside the white filter mask she still wore. Alex smiled at them. He knew it was stupid, and he tried to keep himself from dreaming too far into the future, but Nick was so good with kids; it was hard not to imagine him being a father someday. He and Alex could find a kid who needed a chance, give him or her all the attention and love they had, build a family…

It was a daydream for now, but lately Alex's dreams had been coming true, and he wanted to keep that record going. He should talk to Nick about it at some point and make sure they were dreaming in similar directions.

After some friendly conversation, Nick set the kids back down on the stone terrace. "Come play with us," Damon said, tugging on Alex's hand. "We're building a city."

"In the sandbox," Adrianna added, in case he'd been fooled by Damon's grandiose proclamation.

"Soon," Nick said. Alex watched as he straightened his spine, clearly getting ready for his next greeting. "First, I need to talk to your dad about building something else."

The kids looked curious, but didn't protest, and as they scampered away Nick turned to Alex with doubt clear on his face. "Maybe I shouldn't do it now. If he doesn't like it, he might be an asshole about it, and that'd be bad for everyone."

Alex didn't really have any advice on that front. "Chances are pretty good he'll be an asshole anyway. Your call."

"You're about as reassuring as your sister is," Nick said. He glanced around almost furtively before tugging Alex a few steps to the side. They were behind one of the huge stone pillars that supported the upper deck, and Alex let the memories wash over him. "This is the whole reason I agreed to come to this thing," Nick whispered. "I wanted to lean you up against this pillar, just like the first time…"

"Our first kiss," Alex said with a smile. Then he looked nervously over his shoulder. "Of course, it was the middle of the night then, and we were all alone, not surrounded by family members…"

"And we were soaking wet," Nick said softly, leaning in a little. "You'd taken your shirt off, and your skin was so brown and warm, I couldn't keep my hands off of you…"

"You gave me goosebumps," Alex said. "And I said it was because of the cold."

"And I said you were a liar." Nick closed the rest of the distance between them, and his lips were as soft and sweet as they'd been all those years ago. But there was confidence and control, now, not the confused desperation of their childhood encounter, and Nick kept the kiss more-or-less chaste. There was heat in his eyes when he pulled away, though, and Alex looked forward to further reminiscences at home that night. "Good memories," Nick said. "I'm trying to focus on those."

"You've got a few with your dad, too, I bet."

"Not as many."

"But some. And there's time to build some more." Alex caught Nick's hand. "If you want to. If you don't, then fuck it, let's get out of here. You can visit with Helena and the kids whenever you want, and I can see my family at their place. You don't have to do this, Nick. Not for him, and not for me."

"For me." Nick sounded unsure, but then nodded. "Yeah. I have to give it a chance, so I'll know I did what I could. If it doesn't work, it doesn't work, but... I have to try."

"Do you want me to leave so you can talk to him alone?"

Nick looked startled. "Fuck, no! I want you right here to pull him off me if he goes for my throat."

"I doubt I'll resort to physical violence, Nick."

Nick's eyes widened almost comically as his body froze. Then he turned his head slowly and peered around the edge of the pillar. "Hey, Dad."

"Nick." Blake stepped forward enough that he could see Alex, and Nick eased away so they were all standing at more socially acceptable distances. "Alex. Welcome back, both of you."

"Thanks," they said in unison. Alex felt a nervous laugh burbling up in his chest and tamped it down. This was ridiculous. Maybe he should be intimidated, but Nick? Nick had become a successful businessman in his own right. He'd bested Blake in their recent battle, and then he'd rescued Blake from his own folly. The only reason Blake had a house to host this party in was because Nick had saved his ass. But Nick clearly felt just as awkward and unsure as Alex did.

"Nick," Alex said softly. It was strange to say it in front of Blake, but there they were, and it had to be said. "We're not kids anymore. You're an adult, and you have a business proposal to make."

Nick looked at Alex for a long moment, then nodded. "Yeah," he said. He turned to his father. "I do have a proposal." He grinned suddenly, his face lightening and relaxing into its newly familiar expression of happiness. "For fun, mostly. I'm going to be sticking around Seattle," he let his fingers lace through Alex's in case any explanation was needed, "and I'm looking for something to keep me busy. I was thinking about real-estate development."

"You want to buy the land back from me?" Blake snorted. "For the price I paid for it?"

"Hell, no. I'd have to be stupid to pay that much." Another crazy grin. Nick was back to being himself. "But I thought you might want a partner. You've got the land, and a lot of local contacts. And I know some people who've done well on similar projects in the past. Most importantly, I've still got quite a bit of liquid capital, and I think you could use that." He shrugged and stepped out from behind the pillar. He was still holding Alex's hand, but his fingers were loose and relaxed. "We should talk about it, if you're interested. If you're not, it's not a problem. But I wanted to mention it."

"Partners," Blake said thoughtfully.

"Yeah." Another grin. "We might be a good team. Or we might kill each other. Just thought it'd be interesting to find out."

Blake seemed to be considering the idea. He turned to Alex. "And you'd be involved as well? As corporate counsel, as a businessman in your own right?"

"Neither," Alex said. "This is Nick's game."

"Alex is hanging out his own shingle," Nick said. Alex tried not to smile at the pride he heard in Nick's voice.

"What?" Blake frowned in Alex's direction. "Why?"

"I want to be in charge," Alex replied. He'd given it enough thought to be confident of his reasons. "I want to take the cases *I* want to take, and do pro-bono work when *I* think I can afford it. I want the variety of a smaller firm, instead of specializing in one tiny area of law."

"And he wants to be able to pack up early every now and then without worrying about his boss thinking he's a slacker," Nick added with a grin. Alex knew exactly what Nick planned on doing with Alex's spare time, and he didn't mind at all.

"I see." Blake looked from Nick to Alex and back again. Finally, he shook his head in bemused agreement. "Okay. I'm interested. We should talk." He looked around the backyard gathering, then said, "But not today. Today is about family. And mine is all here, together for the first time. Today, I just want to enjoy that. Okay?"

Nick nodded. "Okay," he said.

Blake squinted at him. "Tomorrow, though… tomorrow we'll talk business."

"Tomorrow," Nick agreed.

"I'm going to go over there and sit down, now," Blake said seriously, pointing. "And I won't be able to see anything happening behind this pillar. But I would like to remind you that there are children in the vicinity…"

"We'll behave ourselves," Alex said quickly.

"Sort of," Nick agreed, and Alex felt himself being whirled around and eased backward against the pillar. "Just a little more," Nick whispered. "I can't get enough of you."

Alex made sure Blake was moving away before he reached out and pulled Nick's mouth to his. The kiss was a little more heated this time, but it was still more of a celebration than the beginning of something passionate. Then again, with Nick, it was hard to draw a firm line between passion and celebration. And that was just the way Alex liked it.

"I love you," Nick murmured into Alex's ear, then trailed kisses along his jawline.

"Always have, always will," Alex replied. He squirmed loose and took Nick's hand. "But we've got lots of time for making out. Lots of time for everything."

"As long as we don't waste any more of it," Nick agreed, and let Alex lead him out to where their families were waiting.

ABOUT THE AUTHOR

KATE SHERWOOD started writing at about the same time that she got back on a horse after a twenty-year break. She'd like to think that she's far too young for it to be a midlife crisis, but apparently she was ready for a few changes!

Her writing focuses on characters and relationships, people trying to find out how much of themselves they need to keep and how much they can afford to give away. She tends to write about dramatic events, but always looks for the humor that helps keep us all sane.

Look for updates at www.katesherwoodbooks.com

ALSO BY KATE SHERWOOD

NOVELS

Dark Horse (Dark Horse Book 1) (also available in Italian and Spanish)

Out of the Darkness (Dark Horse Book 2)

Of Dark and Bright (Dark Horse Book 3)

Trifecta

Lost Treasure

Shying Away (also available as an audio book)

Shining Armor (m/f Romance)

Beneath the Surface

Shadow Valley (m/f Romance, coming October 2012)

NOVELLAS

Home Ice

More Than Chemistry

The Shift

Room to Grow